SEP   2018

D0362447

SEP 2018

ALSO BY
SIRI CALDWELL

DEAL-BREAKER

<u>Angels Series</u>

ANGEL'S TOUCH

EARTH ANGEL

MISTLETOE MISHAP

DRIFTWOOD PUBLIC LIBRARY
801 SW HWY. 101
LINCOLN CITY, OREGON 97367

Mistletoe Mishap
Copyright © 2017 Siri Caldwell

Cover design by Marianne Nowicki

ISBN: 978-0-9974023-3-9 (paperback)
ISBN: 978-0-9974023-2-2 (ebook)

This book is a work of fiction. All names, characters, places, and incidents in this book are the products of the writer's imagination or are used fictitiously. Any resemblance to any persons, living or dead, or to any locales, business establishments, or actual events is strictly coincidental.

All rights reserved. No part of this book may be reproduced or transmitted in any form or by any means whatsoever without written permission of the author, except in the case of brief quotations in critical articles and reviews.

Brussels Sprout Press
P.O. Box 42133
Arlington, VA 22204
United States of America

First edition: November 2017

MISTLETOE MISHAP

SIRI CALDWELL

Brussels Sprout Press

Chapter 1

The deejay had the typical deejay voice, smooth and easy to listen to, the kind of voice that made straight women let men get away with saying outrageous things. Some people found him offensive, but it was hard for Kendra to be offended by much of anything after years of teaching twenty-year-olds who had no filter between their brains and their mouths.

Kendra adjusted the car's passenger-side sun visor against the early-morning glare, angling it so it would help Viv over in the driver's seat. This time of year, when the days grew shorter and the sun dropped lower and lower, this last stretch of highway always made her grateful she wasn't the one driving. She dug through Viv's handbag for her sunglasses and handed them over.

"Here's a listener who sent in a question," the deejay said. "She writes, 'My boyfriend and I are getting married in June. I want to stop having sex until then so it'll be special on our wedding night. My boyfriend thinks this is a bad idea. What do you guys think?'"

"Special?" Viv said in her charming Argentinean accent. "Is she serious?"

"Listeners, please call in if you've ever done something

like this. I need to know what advice to give. So tell me: did holding out make it meaningful?"

Instantly, a caller was on the line. A woman. "I slept at my mother's house the night before the wedding."

"One night?" the deejay scoffed. "Next caller, please. Hi, you're on the air. Did you do this thing? No...shall we say...crossing the line of scrimmage?"

"Yeah," said the male voice.

Wait, what? A man? A man was willing to admit to doing this? And he wasn't afraid someone who knew him might recognize his voice as they drove to work? Clearly Kendra was never going to understand men. Not that she was trying that hard. Or at all.

"My wife wanted me to move out for two weeks prior, to, you know, pretend like we were starting fresh."

Traffic slowed as they drove onto the bridge that led into the city. Kendra curled her fingers around Viv's travel coffee mug sliding in the too-large cup holder, steadying it just in time as Viv let loose a curse and slammed on the brakes, just like every morning. Viv always took the approach too fast.

The deejay's steady stream of chatter continued. "Two weeks. How did she talk you into it, man?"

"Like I had a choice?"

"Two weeks is not a long time," Viv said.

"That's a matter of opinion," Kendra said.

Viv inched the car forward. "What, you're taking his side?"

Kendra shrugged. "Everyone's different. That's all I'm saying."

"Was it worth it?" the deejay asked.

"Sure. Made my wife happy."

"But this woman who's asking for advice is talking about

nada until June. We haven't even hit Christmas yet. That's six months."

"Yeah, six months..." The man's voice trailed off. "That's...yeah."

"Next caller. Hi, you're on the air. You've done this? No scrimmaging for six months?"

"Three months," said the female caller.

"Three months. Excellent." The deejay sounded so cheerful. So positive. So friendly. Like he had *no idea* that listeners stuck in traffic were making rude comments about her. "And you would recommend it to this woman who wrote in?"

"Absolutely. It was wonderful. Women need to know they're special, that it's not something their husband or boyfriend takes for granted."

"I cannot believe these people," Viv said, rolling forward another foot while hugging the bumper of the vehicle ahead of her.

A car horn blared. If Viv had made Kendra wait six months when they'd first met? She couldn't imagine. Back then, being with Viv had been so good...and no, she was not using the word *special*, because yuck...that just thinking about it made her flush hot and cold. Viv's English hadn't been as fluent as it was now, and the sound of her broken voice telling her she loved her had made Kendra's body do horrible, wonderful things Kendra couldn't control. Giving that up for no reason would have been unthinkable.

"It made me really appreciate him and it forced him to talk to me more and connect in ways that didn't involve the bedroom," the caller explained. "Six months sounds amazing."

"She had to *force* him to talk? Poor thing," Viv said.

"Her husband's never having sex again." Kendra took a sip of Viv's coffee and gazed out the window at the rowers defying the morning chill on the river below.

"Drink your own," Viv said.

"Yours tastes better."

Viv sighed. "I asked if you wanted candy cane in yours and you said no."

"It sounded too Christmas-y." Kendra placed the coffee back in the cup holder and adjusted her seatbelt. The end of the bridge was in sight, and their zigzagging route through the city with Viv at the wheel was no place to be guiding a hot drink to her mouth. "That first woman? She'll do it on their wedding night and decide it wasn't all that special after all. She'll say 'Look at what a great relationship we had for the past six months—we don't need to deal with all that physical unpleasantness.' Because if she's willing to hold out for six months, then honestly, she doesn't like it very much."

"Or she's just one of those women who needs to talk before she puts out because it makes her feel closer."

"How much talking does it take to get in the mood?" Kendra said. "Six *months* of talking?" If talking was all it took, then she and Viv would be making out in the car every day, because they were *great* at talking. "They haven't been together long. They're in the honeymoon phase. They should be taking advantage of that before it ends."

Viv waited for a handful of pedestrians to cross so she could make her left turn, the steady click of her blinker a counterpoint to the voices on the radio. For once she wasn't muttering at the stragglers in Spanish to pick up the pace, or questioning their parentage, their life choices, and their footwear. "They're young. They hear people warn them the doing-it-like-bunnies phase will end, but they don't believe it.

They don't think it applies to *them*."

Kendra nodded. Everyone liked to think they were the exception. Much as it pained her to admit, she did the same thing herself. Because those couples who ran out of things to say to each other after a few years? A few decades? That was never going to be her and Viv. Because she and Viv were different. She and Viv were *better* than those couples. She and Viv were *awesome*. "I don't get how putting the bunny action on hold is supposed to make it beautiful, though. Means she thinks it's *not* beautiful right now."

"Maybe it's not."

"I feel sorry for the boyfriend."

"Not the girl?"

"Nah. She's a—"

"Do *not* use that word."

"Did I say that word?"

"You were going to."

"What, a prude?"

"Hey!"

Kendra laughed. "Nah. Just trying to get you riled up." Kendra draped her arm over the driver's seatback and stroked Viv's cheek with the back of her fingers. Viv wasn't a prude. She was just good at hiding it. "We're making fun of these people on the radio, but when was the last time you and I...you know?"

"Made it special?" Viv said the word *special* like it was a word only a thirteen-year-old girl would use, and it was common knowledge that Professor of Immunology Viviana Ortiz had never been thirteen.

Kendra traced Viv's cheekbones. Viv usually shook her off when she did stuff like that in the car, preferring to give her full attention to her driving. Today Viv let her do it, and it felt like a victory.

"Two months?" Kendra guessed, erring in the direction that was less embarrassing.

"Maybe four."

Gah.

Viv captured Kendra's hand and lowered it to Kendra's side of the car with a small, apologetic smile. "Might have that last woman beat."

"Should I call in and break it to them? Say waiting doesn't make it better?"

As the last pedestrian made it across and the light changed to yellow, Viv spun the wheel and sped into the turn. "That'll go over well. I can hear the brides screaming all across the city that you're ruining their special day."

Kendra touched her shoulder, crossing the invisible boundary between their seats. *You're so beautiful*, she wanted to say. When had she become afraid to touch her? She sighed. "Has it really been four months?"

"Maybe?"

"I'm sorry."

"It's both our faults."

Kendra stared at Viv's fingers wrapped around the wheel, capable and experienced, the knuckles bony in a way that gave away her age. She loved Viv's hands. She couldn't remember what they used to look like, back before she'd acquired the smattering of freckles that couldn't already be age spots or the faded, almost invisible scars from the day Viv had been way, wayyyy more upset about the experimental cell culture she'd lost than the shards of broken glassware impaled in her skin. Back when Viv's no-touching-in-the-car rule was one of those things that made her adorable.

Viv was still adorable.

And four months was too long. It might be both their faults, but Kendra was going to fix it.

Chapter 2

Kendra slammed the front door shut to keep the cold air outside where it belonged. Winter wouldn't truly hit DC for another month, but the older she got, the slower her body was to adapt to autumn's dipping temperatures. She let her messenger bag slide off her shoulder and hit the floor. "Does abstinence really make the heart grow fonder?"

"Absence," Viv corrected, shouting from the kitchen. "*Absence* makes the heart grow fonder."

"No, abstinence. I'm thinking—"

"Still thinking about that radio show?" Viv spoke over her.

Either Viv knew her too well or Kendra was becoming predictable.

Probably both.

"Yeah." She nudged her bag with the toe of her boot until it rested against the wall where it wouldn't trip her later. She shoved her keys in her coat pocket, ignoring the cute little hook by the door where Viv's perfectly organized keys dangled, and hung her coat in the entryway closet. "I don't get it. All those people who really, truly believe that not having sex is going to improve their sex lives."

"What?" Viv hollered from the kitchen. "I can't hear

you."

Kendra strolled into the kitchen. "Really? You didn't hear any of that?"

Viv had a pot of water boiling on the stove and was sautéing onions and mushrooms that she poked at with a wooden spoon. "I might have heard a word that starts with the letter *s*, but not the rest of it."

"Anyone would think you taught kindergartners with that mouth, not grad students."

Viv turned down the burner under the frying pan. Kendra watched and held her breath, hoping Viv would kiss her and show her what else she could do with that mouth, but Viv only turned to the cabinet to find the pasta.

Viv opened the box. "Are you going to leave me in suspense?"

"You really didn't hear any of it."

"So tell me again."

"Would a softball coach promise she was going to improve a player's game by benching her for six months?"

"Not the same thing."

"Sure it is. It's a physical skill. How are you supposed to get better at it if you don't practice?"

Viv dropped the pasta into the water. "I wouldn't call it a physical skill. It's more than that."

Kendra popped a sautéed mushroom in her mouth and blew frantically on her fingers to cool them. Viv made a disapproving sound.

Okay, fine. How someone as good at it as Viv was could be so uncomfortable talking about it was beyond her understanding, but if Viv wanted to insist it was all an intellectual and emotional exercise...

"Would a math teacher encourage you to skip class and

not do the homework so that next year, when you move to advanced calculus, you'll enjoy it more?"

Viv grabbed a paper towel and dabbed at her eyes. "Onions."

She was laughing, right?

Kendra stepped out of the kitchen to grab a few tissues and was back a moment later, pressing them into Viv's hands.

Viv blew her nose. "I dare you to call the radio station and tell them more practice is the answer."

"I have a better idea."

"I wouldn't expect any less."

"We're going to test my idea. Using the scientific method."

"The scientific—"

"You're a scientist. I'm sure you've heard of it."

"I have, and I'm pretty sure a sample size of *one* cannot be called *using the scientific method.*"

"I haven't even told you my experiment yet."

"You don't have to. I know what's coming. I can read your mind."

She really could. But Kendra plowed ahead anyway. "The experiment has two arms. In the first arm, we try abstinence. We've already done that, so we don't have to repeat it."

"Let me guess." Viv tapped one finger on her chin like she was thinking hard. She never tapped her chin for real, though. The tapping was an act. "Ooh! I've got it! In the second arm, we try the opposite."

"Are you making fun of me?" Kendra narrowed her eyes. Maybe she could convince Viv she was offended and make her feel guilty.

Viv looked unconvinced. "I'm not making fun of you. I'm making fun of your idea."

"It's a good idea."

"I don't know." Viv turned back to the stove and adjusted the flame under the boiling pasta. "Aren't we already as good as we're going to get? We've had years and years of practice. More's not going to do anything."

Kendra stared at the back of Viv's shoulders. They were slightly rounded, more hunched than they used to be, but she wasn't old, not really. Why would she imply they were too old for this? They still liked each other, right?

Kendra took hold of Viv's apron ties and wound them around her fingers, being careful not to pull and undo the bow drooping at her waist. It was a way to touch Viv without actually touching her, to be near without running the risk of being pushed away.

Kendra didn't do cutesy holiday-themed clothing, but she liked seeing Viv in her Christmas apron, the ties printed in a pattern of holly leaves and berries, because it made Viv happy. The apron and the wreath-embroidered kitchen towels had made their annual appearance a week ago. At school, exams had already started. Soon it would be winter break. Viv would be busy every day in the lab, checking on her racks of culture tubes, monitoring the cells and scary microorganisms inside. They both had to prepare for next semester's classes. But there'd be no classes to teach, no office hours to spend talking with students, no tedious department meetings. They'd have time to be together. Time to watch movies on the sofa and decorate a tree and impede each other's efforts to make dinner. Time to do something about their slump.

But if Viv didn't want to...

Kendra unwound her fingers from Viv's apron ties. It wasn't surprising that Viv would claim she didn't need practice. Viv prided herself on being good at things, and she was good. She'd been good at this particular skill right from the start, long before years of practice had made it nearly impossible for her *not* to be good at it.

So perhaps the better approach was to goad her. Challenge her. Stop appealing to her love of science and make this about proving herself.

"Okay, not an experiment then." Kendra's fingers twitched, wanting to play with Viv's apron ties again but not allowing herself to. Acting pitiful once in a day was more than enough. An idea formed. She expanded her lungs the way she'd been taught a lifetime ago in choir and belted out the line about the partridge in a pear tree. "A competition."

Viv angled her head without turning her body and kissed the underside of Kendra's jaw, somehow managing to keep her wooden spoon safely over the pan where it could drip without making a mess, controlled even without looking. "A singing competition?"

"No. The twelve days of Christmas. The alternative, inappropriate twelve days of Christmas. Competition style." Kendra gently slid the spoon out of Viv's hand and placed it on the ceramic spoon rest. She brushed her lips over Viv's ear and lowered her voice. "Who can make the other person come twelve times first."

"Twelve times sounds a bit excessive," Viv said in her stern, disapproving professor voice.

Kendra put her hands on Viv's hips. Viv didn't squirm away, and the squeezing tension in Kendra's ribcage relaxed. One touch and she felt lighter.

"It has to be twelve, or it's not the twelve days of Christmas." And because once or twice wasn't enough. They needed momentum.

"Twelve times, huh?" Viv turned in her arms. Her lips

were pursed, but a hint of mischief glimmered in her eyes. "That won't take twelve days."

That's my smart girlfriend. My smart, sexy, willing girlfriend. Kendra's smile widened. Viv was going to say yes.

She ran a hand from Viv's hip to her waist to her ribcage. "Only one attempt per day allowed."

"Well…"

Kendra moved higher and lingered on the side of her breast. "What do you think?"

"I…" Viv's breath hitched. "I take it we're doing this on the actual twelve days of Christmas. Or…we could, I suppose. Do the twelve days start on Christmas Day? Or end there?"

Huh. Good question. Were the twelve days even a real thing? She'd always assumed they were a real thing, but… "That's what you're thinking about right now? Logistics?"

"What else would I be thinking about?"

"You're pretty good at doing that blank face thing that you're doing right now. Where you pretend you're not lying." Kendra moved more purposefully over Viv's breast, watching her carefully to make sure Viv didn't want her to stop. "How long do you think you can keep it up?"

Viv's eyes fluttered closed.

Kendra's fingers played over her ribs. "I could make you think about something more fun."

Viv sighed and gently wiggled out of reach.

Yeah. There it was. Moment ended. Kendra sighed, too.

"I need to watch the stove," Viv said.

"Yeah."

"So make me think about having your hands on me later."

Yeah? Okay. Yes. They could do this.

"Make me think about having your *mouth*—" Viv cut herself off before she could finish, because wow, Viv never said things like that. "Or vice versa, I suppose, since I'll be the one winning this competition." She retrieved her wooden spoon and stirred the pot with a controlled calm that made her look anything but controlled and calm. "You never said when the twelve days are."

"You will *not* be winning this…uh…wait, what?" Kendra stammered, struggling to make the mental switch. "Oh. Uh…days. Uh…what's Epiphany? That's the twelfth day, right? January…?"

"Yeah, January sixth. So December twenty-five, twenty-six, twenty-seven…" Viv counted on her fingers.

"Just subtract twenty-five from thirty-one."

"Quiet, I'm counting."

"You're a college professor and you're counting on your fingers?"

Viv ignored her. "Twenty-eight, twenty-nine, thirty…"

"You teach a lab science!"

"So?"

Kendra laughed. "Subtract twenty-five from thirty-one and add one, because you're including both end dates. And add six."

"Thirty-one, one, two…"

Kendra did the math in her head while Viv continued to count on her fingers. "Wait a minute, that adds up to…"

"Three, four, five, six." Viv stared at her hand, which had three fingers curled down with the pinky finger and ring finger sticking out. The ring finger was partly bent and was losing the battle to stay straight, like it was trying its best but was starting to regret having volunteered for this job. "Thirteen."

"That's what I get, too."

Viv uncurled her fingers and started over. "That can't be right. Twenty-five, twenty-six, twenty-seven…"

"Maybe we're not supposed to count Christmas Day."

Viv stopped counting and made a face. "The twelve days of Christmas don't include Christmas?"

"Maybe it's the twelve days *after* Christmas, not *of* Christmas."

"Maybe it's the twelve days *before* Christmas. Like an advent calendar."

"Advent calendars are twenty-four days."

"Are they?"

"I don't know. Aren't they?"

Viv gave a helpless shrug. "They start on December first, right?"

"Who knows." Kendra had never had an advent calendar. She remembered seeing them sometimes at other kids' houses, hanging on their bedroom doors, but did they have twenty-four pieces of chocolate? Twenty-five? No clue. "We're pretty hopeless Christians, aren't we?"

"Speak for yourself. I knew what day Epiphany is."

"But you don't know what it actually means."

"Yeah, but I knew the date. And it *has* to be the twelfth day. It's the only thing that makes sense."

Kendra wrapped her arms around Viv's waist and angled her farther from the sizzling food on the stove to keep her safe. "I don't want to wait until Christmas. I want to start now."

"Grades are due the twenty-sixth. We'd be more relaxed if we started after."

"If we started now, I'd be more relaxed about doing the grading."

Viv gave her a searching look. "You're afraid that if we put it off, we're not going to do it at all, aren't you?"

"Maybe." *Absolutely.* "You really want to wait two weeks?"

"Twenty-four, twenty-three, twenty-two, twenty-one, twenty…" Viv was back to counting on her fingers. "The wait would be only ten days."

"Ten days, two weeks, close enough."

"*Close enough*? I don't know how you geologists make any scientific breakthroughs with that kind of attitude."

"We save our precision for when it matters. Not my fault if the rest of you other scientists are jealous."

"Ten days, two weeks, that's a difference of four days."

"Ooh, she *can* do math in her head."

"Shut up," Viv said with a small smile. "Four days is not nothing."

"It is when you study rocks. A million years is a margin of error."

Viv shook her head, her fingers roaming over Kendra's biceps. "Are you saying I should be happy that you show up anywhere on time?"

"You should be." Kendra's arm warmed under Viv's touch, even through the layer of her sleeve. "And yet ten days without touching you is going to feel like an eternity."

Viv stared at her, searching her eyes as if she needed to figure out whether Kendra was serious or not.

Kendra's chest pinched. Viv should know. Shouldn't she?

Viv leaned in and brushed a kiss on her cheek. "Okay."

"Okay?"

"We can start the challenge now."

Kendra pulled her in tight.

A little burst of laughter escaped Viv's lips, like the

sudden squeeze had taken her by surprise. "Does this hug mean 'Yes, Viv, let's begin?'"

"Yes."

"Maybe it means 'Yes, Viv, you're the best girlfriend I ever had.'"

"That too."

"Lucky for me you can't remember back that far. To the women before me."

Kendra winked. "That's what I tell you, anyway."

Viv gave her a chilly look of warning that probably made her students worry for their grade point average. "That's what you tell me, because it's *true*."

That glare didn't have quite the same effect on Kendra. At least she *hoped* the effect wasn't the same.

"It's true, babe, it's true."

"On your mark, get set—"

"But if Christmas really is only ten days away," Kendra interrupted, "we don't stop at Christmas. We go the full twelve days."

Viv dropped her forehead to Kendra's shoulder with an exaggerated sigh. "It's not the twelve days of Christmas if it neither starts nor ends on Christmas. If we start now, we stop at Christmas."

Oh, now Viv was just playing her.

"Twelve days," Kendra said.

Viv raised her head. "Ten."

"You're cheating me out of two days and we haven't even started yet?"

Viv's mouth twitched, like she was trying not to grin. "I don't have to agree to any of this."

"But you want to."

"Do I?"

"Twelve days." Seriously. Kendra was not backing down on this.

"If we include today and we include Christmas Day, that's…" Viv double-checked on her fingers. "…eleven."

Was that supposed to be a compromise? "You're welcome to stop at eleven, but that means you automatically forfeit."

"Not if we change the rules."

"We're not changing the rules."

"Whoever can make the other person come eleven times first."

Kendra laughed. "I don't think so."

Viv kissed her on the cheek and wiggled out of her arms to rescue their dinner before it burned. "We could talk about this all night. Or someone could say *ready, set*—"

"Go."

Chapter 3

Day 1

KENDRA 0 : VIV 0

Kendra clicked off the bedroom light and hauled herself into bed in her sleep shirt and bare legs, hiking one hip onto the mattress and rolling because the bed was too tall for her to sink onto it gracefully. She got under the covers, and Viv yanked the edge of the sheet back into place, pulling it up to her chin.

"Sorry I didn't get you a partridge, seeing as how it's the first day of Christmas," Kendra said. Not the officially correct first day—they weren't going to figure out when exactly that was—but *their* first day. "Or a pear tree."

"Thank God for small favors," Viv said in the dark.

"Hey! Where's your sense of romance?"

Kendra found her with her cold feet and Viv squirmed away.

"I have no sense of romance when it comes to taking care of pet birds. No one should ever give an animal as a gift."

"Yeah, yeah. It's not fair to the person or the animal. I know. A really good friend of mine explained it to me once. Or twice. Or three ti—"

"Gardening's also a lot of work," Viv said. "Giving someone a fruit tree is—"

"It's just a song, babe." Viv was thoughtful and practical and cared about things like protecting pear trees and partridges from neglect, and Kendra loved that about her, but there was such a thing as being *too* practical. "No one's asking you to plant a pear tree."

"I know, but—"

"Just wait until you see the seven swans I ordered. You're going to love them. They're beautiful and classy and the breeder *swears* they take care of themselves."

Viv sighed. "You're lucky I can tell when you're joking."

"The only issue is rounding them up and getting them into the car when it's time to take them to the vet for their vaccinations. Supposedly they hiss."

"You're ridiculous."

"And sexy."

Viv huffed a laugh. "Possibly."

Kendra turned onto her side and nudged her thigh between Viv's legs. They were both tired, both ready to stop talking and move on to knocking day one of the countdown off the list.

They rocked in a slow, familiar rhythm, gently working their bodies closer together. Kendra got lost in it, lulled by their sleepy pace and the warmth of Viv's body. There was no urgency in it, just the comfort of holding each other. She could happily fall asleep like this.

"I think I forgot to take the last load of laundry out of the washer." Viv's voice knocked her awake.

Please don't get up. Kendra knew what was coming next: Viv was going to get out of bed. *Please don't go check the washer.*

"I should check. I don't want our clothes to be damp all night. They'll mildew."

"The washer's empty."

Viv rolled onto her back, her warmth slipping away as their legs disengaged. "I don't remember emptying it."

No. Stay. Stay here. "I did it. I ran the dryer." And thank God she had.

"You did?"

"Yup." Kendra reached for her and tangled their legs together again. *Stay. We have to do day one. We have a plan.*

"Oh good." Viv snuggled closer, then froze.

Crap. Viv was thinking again.

"You sure?" Viv asked.

"I'm sure. Folded everything and put it away."

"Oh. Thanks." Viv squeezed Kendra's thigh between her own in a lower-body thank-you hug. "That was nice of you."

Did everyone do this? Discuss household chores while their bare legs were intertwined? In the same exact everyday tone of voice they'd use on the phone at work in front of coworkers? Did they find themselves paying more attention to the question of whether they had, in fact, remembered to do the laundry, than to the sensation of skin against skin?

When had she started taking that sensation for granted? It was a miracle that she got to be with Viv naked and share a bed with her every night. When she remembered what it had been like to wonder if she was the only teen in the world who felt this way about girls and how she'd worried she might never find someone to love, this conversation seemed impossible. She should be shaking with excitement that Viv would touch her at all. When did she lose that? Why hadn't she noticed?

"I guess we should be talking about something more romantic," Viv said.

"Like how fun it will be to do this for twelve days," Kendra agreed. Twelve, not eleven. Kendra had won that argument over dinner.

"I just needed to clear my mind. To stop worrying."

"Sure thing. All cleared now?"

Viv made a noncommittal sound. "The minute I relax about one thing, I remember something else to feel stressed about."

"Let me distract you then." Kendra found Viv's shoulder in the dark and stroked softly down her arm. Up and down and up…and down…and up…and…

Crap. Kendra had almost fallen asleep there.

Distract her, she reminded herself. *Don't put us both to sleep.*

"You still awake?" Kendra asked.

Viv's breathing was quiet and even.

Too quiet. Too even.

Shit.

Chapter 4

Day 2

KENDRA 0 : VIV 0

While her students crammed last-minute studying into every free moment not spent taking exams, Kendra was in her lab inventorying supplies, ordering what she needed for next semester, and testing her lab equipment—the twenty polarizing microscopes, the two rock saws, the rock polisher, and all the other fun stuff—to ensure everything was working. Today had been a full day of repairing what had been battered by a semester of use.

By the time she finished, she was more than ready to walk over to Viv's building to meet up with her in the Madison Activity Room for the end-of-semester party—more correctly referred to as the school-wide faculty/staff/alumni winter holiday celebration, informally known as the why - do - I - have - to - go - to - these - things - I - have - nine - other- Christmas - parties - on - my - schedule - in - the - next - two - weeks extravaganza—and stuff herself with hors d'oeuvres. And possibly red or green desserts.

She wasn't one of those people who hated socializing with her coworkers. She liked her coworkers. She liked catching up with former students who weren't too old yet to wear plush reindeer antlers and jingle bell earrings, and she liked listening to the university a cappella group perform. It would be a nice change from working alone in silence all day.

And when she spotted Viv stealing a sprig of mistletoe from the festive decor, she realized they'd stayed long enough.

Kendra took Viv by the elbow and guided her out into the empty hallway, the roar of voices not muted in the least by the open double doors.

"One down," Kendra said, confident that Viv would know what she was talking about. "Eleven to go."

Viv smirked. "One down, *ten* to go."

Oh good. She knew. But what the heck was she trying to pull now?

Viv knew it wasn't ten. She was just being difficult. Perhaps because she had this weird idea that it turned Kendra on. Perhaps because it did.

"Today is day two. I don't know why you're having trouble with the math, but like I said, if you'd like to forfeit, feel free."

"Me? Forfeit? I plan to win." Viv put one hand on her hip and imitated Kendra's *just-you-watch-me* wiggle, with plenty of shoulder and booty action.

It looked ridiculous on her.

Ridiculously adorable.

And to see her do it within earshot of a work function, where someone could walk out at any moment and see her, was amazing.

Kendra shivered. Losing would not be a hardship.

But she wasn't going to lose.

"You can *plan* to win all you want," Kendra said. "Doesn't mean it's going to happen."

"But it will."

"Doubt it."

"In six days, you'll see how wrong you are."

"Eleven days."

"Six. Or five, plus today. Since we didn't have a winner yesterday, all I have to do is win the next six times, and I've won the whole thing."

Viv looked way too excited about this.

"I see what you're doing, babe, but let's review: The bet was *not* whoever wins fifty-one percent of the twelve days first. It was whoever could make the other person..." Kendra cleared her throat. The hallway looked empty, but she wasn't going to say *come*. "...twelve times first."

"Which was not logically sound. How can either of us get twelve wins if we can only try once a day? We're already down to only ten days."

"Eleven."

"Which is also less than twelve."

Shit, Viv was right. They hadn't thought this through.

"I can't believe this." If they didn't change the rules, they'd both already lost.

"Majority wins," Viv said.

"No." There was no way Viv was going to lock her out early and cheat them out of the last...five?...days of competition. No way. "Whoever can make the other person..." Oh dear God, she was turning into Viv, unable to say certain words out loud, but Jesus, *everyone* she worked with was inside that room. She coughed. "The most times."

"Which will be clear after six wins."

Kendra shook her head. "You're forgetting there could be more than one winner per day. We could *both* rack up eleven wins by the end of this."

"Oh." Viv bit her lip and her eyes grew rounder, making her look twenty years younger. "Right. I knew that."

Kendra kissed Viv's forehead. "Ready to have your mind

blown eleven more times?"

"*More* times? You mean *times*."

"I've done this before," she whispered into her hair. "To you. I'm sure you remember."

Viv flushed. "Possibly."

"I saw you take that mistletoe."

Viv looked down at the snip of drooping greenery she'd been hiding behind her back.

"Have plans for it?" Kendra asked.

"I have no idea what you mean."

Kendra laughed. "Sure you don't."

That mistletoe was *Viv's* idea, not Kendra's. That was a really good sign. It meant Viv wasn't going to be jumpy when it came time to use it.

"If I did—and that's a big *if*—it would require a change of venue."

"A change of venue," Kendra said. "You mean, like the restroom down this hall?"

"Ugh, no."

At the far end of the hallway, a woman from Kendra's department turned the corner and came their way, no doubt heading for the party. The absurd reindeer antler headgear kind of gave it away. Viv not-so-subtly pretended to examine the nearest of the display cases that lined the walls, highlighting notable events in the school's history.

"I know her," Kendra hissed.

"Shit," Viv whispered. Her expression shifted subtly and her voice resumed a conversational level. "How did everything go in the lab today? Did you have to realign the rock saw again?"

"Always," Kendra said, slightly irritated that Viv could make the switch so seamlessly. And slightly mollified that she understood her work. Cutting rocks into slices was unsurprisingly hard on the saw blades, and hammering a rim to shape it by a few thousandths of an inch was tricky. "The blade was getting jammed in the cut, as usual."

"Kendra!" said her colleague Lashanna as she approached. "Are you on your way in or planning your escape?"

Kendra smiled. "Escape? You mean that's an option?"

"Who's going to tell? Not me." Lashanna glanced curiously at Viv, who had turned to nod politely at her.

Lashanna was a new hire, and it was obvious she had either never met Viv or didn't recognize her, so Kendra made the introductions.

"You two should come to my Christmas cookie-decorating party," Lashanna said.

"Uh…" Kendra said eloquently.

"I always have one for my girls, but this year I thought, why should the kids have all the fun?"

Fun?

"That's very kind of you," Viv said. She was always careful with the way she spoke, but in professional situations, when she tried to hide the foreign accent she'd never completely been able to lose, her diction became excruciatingly correct.

"Yeah, thanks for the invite," Kendra said. "But I don't think we're in the cookie-decorating spirit this year." *Because we have alternate plans for every single day between now and Christmas.*

Lashanna gave a don't-worry-about-it wave of her hand. "I know what you mean."

God, Kendra hoped not.

"Well. I should go face the chaos in there," Lashanna said, indicating the open doors to the holiday party.

"And we need to make our getaway," Kendra said. "If anyone asks if you saw me…"

Lashanna nodded. "I'll tell them you were full of festive cheer."

"No!" Kendra said, but Lashanna was already leaving. "They'll never believe *that*."

"I might have seen you wearing reindeer antlers," Lashanna said over her shoulder, grinning.

"How do people know this shit about me?" Kendra complained to Viv once they were alone. "She's only worked here one semester."

"People talk."

"About my opinion on something completely irrelevant like Christmas accessories?"

Viv twisted the mistletoe between her fingers. "Are we really going home? I thought we were only taking a break out here. I thought you were required to attend."

"I'm required to make an appearance," Kendra said.

She didn't like the residue of formality in Viv's voice.

Don't change your mind, don't change your mind, don't change your mind, Viv, babe, please.

"Which I did," Kendra said. "So did you."

Viv pressed her lips together, clearly torn. "I did, didn't I."

"Yes, you did. That means we're both done for the night as far as work responsibilities go."

Viv looked like she was thinking about it.

She ought to be. She was the one with the mistletoe, after all.

"You know," Kendra said, "I seem to remember your office is conveniently located in this very building." Down a maze of endless hallways, but still. "That would definitely be closer."

"It would," Viv agreed.

"Yeah?" Kendra suddenly felt a lot more cheerful.

"Yeah. Come on."

———

The immunology department's hallway was decked out for the holidays, walls and office doors covered in paper snowmen, snowflakes, and poinsettias.

Viv stopped at an electrical outlet outside a dark office and unplugged a string of colored lights. "We're supposed to turn these off when we leave for the night."

"Doesn't the night security guard do that?" Kendra glanced down the empty hallway. This wasn't the only door that remained festively lit. "And you didn't tell me your department had a nondenominational holiday door-decorating contest." Amazing that with all the hours they spent talking, there were still tidbits that never got mentioned. Apparently it was very important that Kendra be aware of the pros and cons of the various sizes of glassware Viv used in the lab, but this door thing was so uninteresting to Viv that it hadn't even occurred to her to bring it up.

"How did you figure out it was a contest?"

"I'm smart that way." She pointed to the door on their left. A snowman was doubled over, spewing fluorescent green…was that oatmeal? A photo taken through a microscope of a disgusting parasite was glued to its belly. She'd bet anything the professor behind that door was a specialist in that disease and had personally taken that pic. "Immunologist humor?"

"Neville does this every year. You don't remember?"

"I only care about one thing in your department, and it's not Professor Vomit."

"Aw. Sweet, but I know you're just oblivious."

"I'm not oblivious. To you."

Viv gave her a look. "Each year he switches the patient. Last year it was a penguin. The year prior to that, it was a polar bear." She bent down and unplugged another string of lights. "He finds it amusing that students might believe a cold-weather animal would be infected by a tropical disease."

"Charming."

"Unfortunately, someone in a position of power on some unnecessary departmental committee found his enthusiasm for the season inspirational." Viv finished with the lights and straightened. "And then we all had to do it."

"I thought you liked decorating for Christmas," Kendra said, trailing behind Viv as they continued walking. "You do it at home."

"I don't like being *forced* to decorate. I prefer to do it because I *want* to."

They were almost at Viv's office. From a distance, it didn't look like she'd done anything to her door. There were no dangling lights, no wreath jutting out.

"My students wanted to help," Viv said. "I told them they should be studying for their exams, but they were very insistent."

"They love you."

"They don't love me."

"Give it a rest, Viv. Your students know a good thing when they see it."

"My students know a good excuse to avoid studying when they see it. So I decided on something that required minimal effort."

"Can't wait," Kendra said.

A few more steps, and there it was. Viv had covered her door in black wrapping paper and stuck a small circle of red foil in the center, two-thirds of the way up. At the very top were the words RUDOLPH IN THE DARK.

"I love it." Kendra checked out the door across the hall—a pinecone wreath—and turned back to Viv's door with her hands on her hips. "This is so you. You say decorating is a waste of time, you hate that the school forces you to do it, you watch your slacker coworker hang a plain old wreath, and then you come up with this."

"I borrowed the idea. It wasn't mine."

"Doesn't mean I can't like it."

"One of the kids wanted to rig up a battery-powered flashing red LED for the nose but didn't get around to it." Viv crossed her arms. "Because I reminded her to study."

"No, this is better." An LED would've ruined it. It wouldn't have been Viv. It would've made it seem like she cared about something other than the scientific rigor of her experiments. "Did you win the contest?"

"You know I'm not competitive about anything but my work."

"Oh, please." Viv was competitive about everything.

"I'm not."

"I want a photo."

Kendra pulled out her phone and waved Viv into position in front of her door. Viv's grumpy ass-kicking frown gave way to embarrassment, but she stood where Kendra wanted her, strenuously avoiding making eye contact. Kendra snapped the photo anyway. Then Viv looked up through her lashes, hands behind her back, and Kendra got a second shot, and wow, was it worth the wait, because sweet Jesus did Viv look hot when she mixed shy with defiant.

"You're not going to tell me Rudolph isn't religion-neutral?"

"Unlock your door, Viv, before I ravish you in the hallway in front of Rudolph."

Viv took her time opening the door before flipping on the lights and leading her inside. Kendra shut the door behind them. There didn't seem to be a way to lock it from this side, but that was okay. It was late, the students were on break, and the cleaning crew had left for the night.

"Wouldn't want to scar innocent little Rudolph," Viv said from behind her, close to her ear.

Viv took her by the shoulders, mistletoe still clutched in one fist, and kissed the back of her neck. Kendra let her head drop forward. Her mind blanked for a moment. She lived for this: Viv's closeness, her warm breath, the gentle press of her chest against her back.

"Better?" Viv asked softly.

"Much." Kendra turned in her arms. "Don't lose that mistletoe. I'm going to need you to hold it over your head now."

"Why? You going to kiss me?"

Kendra kissed her cheek. "I'm going to convince you to let me ravish you on your desk."

Viv released her. "My desk? No."

They both turned and eyed the desk.

"Why not?"

"That wouldn't…actually…work." Viv paused. "Would it?"

"Are you thinking about it?" No one would guess Viv would be the type, and usually Viv wasn't, but Kendra knew she had it in her. "*I'm* thinking about it."

"But it's so awkward."

"So convenient, you mean." She could have Viv on her back and Kendra could kneel between her legs and...yeah. Her face felt a little warm just thinking about it. The hard linoleum floor would be hell on her knees, but it might be worth it.

Viv's desk, like everything in the building aside from the computers and the scientific equipment, was ancient. Under all her paperwork and her computer and her scattered pens and paperclips and office mug was good solid wood construction that could easily support the weight of two middle-aged women. But was it too tall? If she was on her knees, the desk surface would be, what, chest height? Shoulder height? And then with Viv lying on top of it, that would be even higher.

Was she really doing this? Mentally measuring the desk's height?

"Convenient for work," Viv said. "Not for...you know."

"Convenient for a multitude of purposes."

"Which do not include ravishing."

"We'll see about that."

"It's unhygienic," Viv protested.

Kendra laughed. They both knew that whatever they did here, it wasn't going to go any further than a kiss. Maybe a little groping. But that didn't mean they couldn't consider this desk scenario.

"I remember you dragging me into a public restroom more than once, Little Miss Unhygienic. And did I complain? No, I did not." That had been years ago, but Viv hadn't changed all that much. If she could make out with her in an endless row of muddy stalls at a football stadium, and in a ladies' room in a hushed science museum where used paper towels overflowed the trash receptacle, and at an abandoned highway rest stop that smelled extremely questionable, she could do it here.

"We were upright," Viv said. "And we kept all our clothes on."

"So you are giving this some thought. Considering the mechanics?"

"Enough to know it would be physically uncomfortable."

True. The back of Viv's head on the desk would not be comfortable. Kendra's knees on the floor with no rug and no pillow would not be comfortable. "Comfort's not everything."

"Don't forget inconvenient. It's not *your* precisely positioned computer monitor that we'd have to move."

"I think your problem is, you don't want me to sweep your papers off your desk." Kendra lowered her forearm to the edge of the desk to demonstrate. She wasn't going to actually do it, of course. Messing up Viv's paperwork would be mean. Teasing her, however…

"Kendra. Don't. Don't even think about it." Viv dropped the mistletoe on the desk and slammed her hands on the two piles closest to Kendra's arm, pinning them in place.

Kendra raised her hands, palms out in surrender. "Babe. You know I wouldn't."

"Sorry." Viv raised her hands, too, mirroring her. "I know that." She dropped her arms to her sides. "I'm not much of a romantic, am I?"

"You do okay."

Viv straightened her paperwork. "How is an adult supposed to fit on an office desk, anyway? The short way is too short and the long way is…" She quirked her head to assess the desk's length. "…also too short."

"I guess if we were high-powered executives we'd have

bigger desks."

"We should measure."

A couple of minutes ago, I was thinking the same exact thing.
Except that Viv's idea of measuring was going to be a lot
more work than Kendra's. She just knew it. "We really don't
need to."

"I used to have a yardstick in here somewhere. Maybe it's
still here."

Yup. More work. More precise than eyeballing, which
was all Kendra had needed. But that was Viv.

"Babe. Your desk is safe from sex cooties. Okay? You
don't have to measure. No need to prove anything."

"But now I'm curious."

So adorable. So...intellectual. Not that Kendra wasn't
intellectual, too, but she knew when to turn it off.

Viv opened a supply cabinet and pulled out a yardstick.
Of course she did.

"Ah, it's metric." Viv looked pleased. She laid her
*meter*stick on the table and aligned it with the edge.

"Really, Viv, this is—"

"Romantic?"

"Not really."

"You don't find measurement romantic? What kind of
scientist are you?"

"The kind who doesn't care whether that thing is in
metric. Because we did not come to your office at almost
midnight to measure your desk."

"You don't care what units I'm using? I'm shocked.
Because I suspect you're the kind who's very interested in the
result." Viv bent over her desk as she moved the meterstick
to the other edge to continue measuring. She bent quite a bit
more than necessary. She might have even wiggled her tail

feathers.

Wait. Viv was into this? She wasn't mad anymore?

"You know what kind of scientist I am?" Kendra said. "The kind who's about to steal your mistletoe."

Viv lunged for the mistletoe, fumbling the meterstick and knocking it clattering to the floor in her haste, but Kendra got to the greenery first. She dangled it above Viv, straightening her arm and stretching as high as she could. Viv reached and tried to push it away so it wouldn't be overhead, and their hands tangled together, fighting for dominance.

"Afraid it's going to drop germs on your head?" Kendra teased.

"Afraid it's going to give you ideas."

They were both about the same height, so the only way for Viv to have any chance of winning was for her to press as close to Kendra as possible. But Viv wasn't plastered to her. Which was disappointing.

"What kind of ideas?"

"Ideas about what people do underneath that stupid vine you're dangling over my head."

"Me?" Kendra rose higher on her toes, ankles wobbling to keep her balance. It would be embarrassing to fall. "I'm calculating the angle you need. I'm thinking if our bodies form two sides of a triangle that meet at our hands, and both sides are the same distance, how small does the angle have to be for you to—"

"This small," Viv said, pressing the entire length of her body to Kendra's, slotting their breasts side by side so her mouth was directly by Kendra's ear. Finally. "A zero-degree angle."

"There you are." Kendra wrapped her free arm around Viv's waist, trapping her. She could feel the rise and fall of

Viv's chest where it pressed against her own, and something inside her relaxed on a level that only Viv could access.

Viv's lips brushed against her ear. "You think I fell into your trap, don't you."

Kendra shivered. "Yeah."

Viv was still reaching overhead with one arm, not giving up on the mistletoe, which meant her silky sweater and the camisole underneath it were riding up, and Kendra found bare skin without even having to work for it.

Viv faltered, making a sound that was more than a little turned on. She clung one-handedly to Kendra's shoulder, either for balance or for leverage to reach higher.

Kendra nearly relaxed her arm.

And why shouldn't she? Why shouldn't she drop the mistletoe? She'd already gotten what she wanted.

It would mean Viv would win, though.

But it was hard to care.

Kendra gave up the fight, dropping to her heels as Viv claimed the mistletoe and kissed her cheek. Kendra used both hands to hold Viv's waist, pulling their hips flush. She could feel Viv's smile against her skin.

"I thought you said you didn't want me getting any ideas," Kendra said.

The mistletoe tumbled from Viv's fingers to the floor as she cupped the nape of Kendra's neck, cradling her, and licked under her jaw.

Kendra groaned, louder than was probably wise, the force of her body's reaction taking her by surprise. She angled her head to give Viv better access.

This.

This was what she missed.

Viv mouthed at a spot underneath her jaw, lingered on

Kendra's bare throat, and kissed her way down her neck.

Kendra's knees weakened. "Viv, oh my God, I would've given you the mistletoe if I'd known you were going to—"

"Professor?" A man's voice came from outside the door. "You still working?"

Viv went rigid in her arms, her grip suddenly too tight.

Shit. Didn't people know they were supposed to go home at night and not live in the lab?

Slowly, silently, Viv unclenched her fingers and released her.

"Who is that?" Kendra whispered across the tiny bit of space that now separated them. If he was one of her students, Viv might recognize his voice.

"Security," Viv whispered back. Then she called to the guard, raising her voice. "Yes. Of course. Late night."

Viv made no move toward the door. That meant she and this guy weren't in the habit of making conversation, right? Otherwise she'd go open the door and talk to him. Or he'd open it himself to check on her. The stupid door which stupidly did not lock from the inside.

Kendra felt a sudden urge to giggle and clamped her hand over her mouth.

"Don't forget to go home," the guard said.

"I won't," Viv replied. "Have a good night."

At the sound of his retreating footsteps, Kendra let her laughter escape in quiet gasps that she muffled against Viv's shoulder.

"That wasn't funny," Viv said, petting Kendra's hair with the familiar soothing rhythm that helped calm Kendra down at night when she couldn't sleep, but sometimes turned her on instead.

Like now, for example.

"He wouldn't have seen anything embarrassing," Kendra said, nuzzling into Viv's hand to encourage the petting action. "We have clothes on."

"Thank God for small favors."

"I don't know that I'd call it a *favor*…"

Viv shook her head in bemusement. "You know what I look like. You see me without clothes all the time."

"Never gets old, though." Kendra looked her up and down with an exaggerated eyebrow wiggle.

Viv rolled her eyes. Every time Viv got that look on her face, like she couldn't decide whether she was exasperated by Kendra or charmed, Kendra fell even more in love with her.

She smoothed her thumb across Viv's cheekbones and traced her lips. The need to kiss her was overwhelming. "Want to try this again?"

Viv gave her a considering look, then sighed and gestured to the industrial-size wall clock hanging above her door. "Look at the time."

"What, you're tired?"

Viv shook her head. "Midnight. Day two is over, and we both lost. Again."

"One minute past midnight," Kendra corrected, unwilling to believe Viv was serious. "Now it's day three. We can do this. We can do anything we want."

"I think I can guess what *you* want."

"Yup. And this time, I'm going to win."

Chapter 5

Day 5

KENDRA 0 : VIV 0

Day three had *not* begun with Viv bent over her desk. Instead, too rattled by the security guard's visit, they'd gone home and fallen asleep. Day four was also a bust. Seriously, those bird days were cursed. The partridge, the doves, the hens, the mockingbirds…no…calling birds? Never heard of a calling bird. Or a French hen, for that matter. Or even a partridge. Come on, people, this was America. The fruited plains and purple mountain majesties weren't soaring with highfalutin birds that sang with a French accent.

But now those bird days were over, and things were going to turn around. Five golden rings…that sounded promising. And then six…

…geese.

Damn it. Couldn't get away from those birds. Six geese, seven swans…it was like the birds were getting bigger and bigger and meaner and meaner, and who gave their true love a goose, anyway? Those things were vicious.

The college's wide green lawns attracted huge mobs of Canada geese in winter, and also in summer, because the birdbrains had discovered it was easier to camp out down south all year long than to bother with the whole migration thing. Left more time and energy for more important activities like pooping and hissing at absentminded faculty who dared get too close.

So…rings. The only thing in the whole nonsensical song that was in any way related to romance.

Not really, though. Viv said rings were shiny petri dishes, and she couldn't wear one in the lab anyway because it would snag on the gloves she wore to protect her from the viruses she worked with. Kendra didn't wear one either, because wedding rings reminded her too much of straight people. A friend who taught gender studies had once complimented the two of them on resisting the symbols of the patriarchy, but it wasn't about that. Not unless simply being themselves and defining their relationship by their own rules was an act of political resistance. Which maybe it was? Gah. There was a reason she'd never studied the humanities beyond the required minimum.

So…not rings. They'd have to come up with something that wasn't a hazard in the lab and didn't force Kendra to confront her political beliefs, and then they'd have to get serious about this competition because the song was about *day* five, not *night* five, and here it was time for bed already. They'd blown most of the day working, driving in to pick up their students' exams and spending the rest of the day catching up on paperwork. Which did need to get done, but come on. If she wanted to win—if she wanted either one of them to win—they might have to reconsider their priorities.

Kendra undressed while Viv read in bed, waiting for her. Viv was wearing her reading glasses and her white flannel pajamas with the red candy canes buttoned all the way to her neck, looking all intellectual and untouchable. Kendra watched her out of the corner of her eye, but Viv never looked up.

Of course she didn't. Kendra couldn't remember the last time Viv had watched her undress. If she ever had. She didn't know if Viv ignored her because she was being polite and proper and trying to give her privacy or because she wasn't that interested in looking at her body. And wasn't that mildly depressing. Even though she knew Viv wasn't critical. And even though Kendra considered herself to be the kind of person who looked better in clothes than out of them. To be honest, *most* people looked better in clothes than out of them.

She liked watching Viv, though.

She didn't understand why Viv didn't like to watch her.

The times Viv undressed in front of Kendra and caught Kendra watching, she seemed amused. Occasionally she'd even flaunt it a little, in an extremely subtle, not shy but barely detectable, Viv-like way. But then she'd hop into the shower or change into whatever clothes she was changing into and that was the end of it, no kiss or anything, and Kendra would tell herself it was enough.

She hadn't understood, when she was younger, that she could be so stupidly in love with someone that she could be irritated with her and want her at the same time.

"I think we need to come up with new words to this song," Kendra said.

Viv glanced up from her book. "Six geese a-laying aren't doing it for you?"

"Oh, now we're skipping days? Again? We're on five golden rings, babe. No cheating us out of a day."

"I was under the impression that a single day was negligible to a geologist, seeing as how a million years is a margin of error."

This was what she got for falling for a smart chick. She should have known Viv wasn't going to forget that comment.

"Nice try, but I know what day it is." Kendra crawled onto the bed naked. "I'm pretty sure you do, too."

Viv turned the page of her book and ignored her.

"I can see your lips twitching," Kendra said. "I know you're trying hard not to laugh at how hilarious you are, pretending you don't see me."

"I'm not pretending."

"Yes you are."

"Am not."

"Are too. You can't resist me." Kendra stalked closer. "You're my true love and I'm your true love, and on the fifth day of Christmas we're going to prove our love with five ring alternatives, and they are…"

Viv let her reading glasses slide down the bridge of her nose and leveled a forbidding gaze at her from over top of the rims. "Six cheesy come-ons."

"I knew you were paying attention." Kendra stayed on her hands and knees, waiting for Viv to give some sign that she'd noticed what Kendra was not wearing. "But don't think you're scamming anyone into skipping day five."

"I wouldn't dream of it."

"So on day five you're giving me…?"

"You know I believe in good sportsmanship, and good sportsmanship means taking turns. It wouldn't be fair for me to suggest lyrics for day five when I just did day six. It's your turn."

"Fine." Kendra thought about the tune. Days six through twelve were all the same unfinished pattern, like a record skipping and repeating itself until you screamed at your brother to move that needle now, goddammit, or I'll tell Mom where you were last Saturday when she thought you were at soccer practice. Day five was the big line where you got to belt out the words and prove you had the singing voice of a star. She had to come up with something good.

Got it. She sat on her heels and took a breath and sang. "Six cheesy come-ons." Another breath. "Miiiind-blowing sex."

"Ooooh." Viv sounded impressed.

In an I'm-just-humoring-you, was-I-supposed-to-be-turned-on, oh-I-think-I-*was* kind of way.

Because she was a little shit.

Who was going to be jumping out of those candy cane pajamas in the very near future and losing day five. And liking it.

"Your turn," Kendra said.

Viv sang quietly, a little off-key like she always was on the rare occasions she forgot to be self-conscious about her voice. "Four enticing smiles."

Kendra loved hearing her relax enough to sing. She knew better than to call attention to it, though, or Viv would clam up.

"Smiles? That's all you've got?"

Viv tilted her book down so it lay flat on her lap. "What? Smiles are sexy."

"Jesus Christ. Smiles are the least sexual thing that could possibly, under the right circumstances, be construed as sexual."

"Probably shouldn't be taking the Lord's name in vain while singing about His holy birth."

"Like you ever set foot inside a church."

"My parents dragged me to church a lot more often than yours did."

"I went. I sang in the choir."

"And learned so much. *I'm* the one who knew what day

Epiphany is."

Kendra dropped to the comforter and rolled to her side. She groaned. "This again?"

"Can't wait to hear what shockingly sexual thing you're going to make me sing for day three."

Kendra smirked. "Three kiss...es."

"Two unbuttoned shirts," Viv sang primly, flipping another page in her book like a jerk. She clearly had not been reading, so there was no way she needed to turn the page.

"You know how it turns me on when you look all intellectual."

"Is that one of our six cheesy come-ons for today?"

Today? Seriously? "For *tomorrow*," Kendra corrected. Viv did look hot, though. "Is it working?"

"No." Viv continued to stare at her book as one hand moved to her neckline and played with the top button of her pajama top. Acting like she was doing it absentmindedly, she slipped the button free. Like she had no idea what her hand was doing. Like she wasn't paying attention to anything but the words on the page.

While Kendra was *naked*.

"I think we need to change the rules," Viv said.

"Do we, now. Why?" Kendra pushed herself up from the mattress and leaned on her elbows, still on top of the comforter even though Viv was under it, warming the sheets. "Because I'm winning?"

"You're not winning. You have zero points. I have zero points. It's a tie."

"Not for long."

Viv removed her reading glasses and set them on her bedside table with a familiar clink. "Why? Because in a little while, you'll have one point and I'll have one point? It will remain a tie."

"I'll make you come first. Then I'll be ahead," Kendra said, because no way was she going to concede that Viv might have identified a flaw in their plan. *Another* flaw.

"And then it will be my turn, and it will again be a tie." Viv moved her pillows, getting ready to settle under the covers, her book sliding off her lap. "It's unwinnable. The way it's set up, at midnight it will always be a tie."

"Not if I run out the clock."

Viv paused. Carefully, she repositioned her pillows, wedging them behind her back as she scooted up to sit, punching them into shape like it was their fault she'd changed her mind about lying down.

Wait. Had she really been planning to sleep? Right now?

The book went back onto Viv's lap. She opened it without looking. "What are you saying, you planned out a strategy? You're going to watch the minutes count down until midnight while you're…you know?"

"While I'm…what?" Kendra teased.

"You know."

"Making you lose?"

"Yes," Viv ground out.

"I can't tell if you're more upset about the idea of me pulling ahead in the scores or about me paying attention to the time and not giving you my undivided attention."

"Hmm." Viv undid another button on her pajamas.

"Is this…revenge flirting?" Kendra asked.

"We need to change the rules," Viv insisted.

"To what?"

Viv dipped her chin and gazed up at her from beneath her lashes as she undid one more button. "I don't know yet."

Kendra eyed the thermostat, but couldn't read it from

this distance. Was it set right? Because the bedroom didn't need to be *this* warm.

"Or," Kendra suggested, "we could leave the rules exactly as they are." She watched Viv fondle the buttonhole she'd freed one-handedly, her other hand resting on her book. "And I could make it so good that you conk out and fall asleep right after."

"You're the one who falls asleep right after," Viv countered.

"So there you go. Your chance to win."

"Hmm. I suppose."

"Not that you're *going* to win."

"Is that right." Viv took a breath, subtly expanding her ribcage and causing the two sides of her pajama top to fall slightly open.

Well yeah, they both knew Viv could turn Kendra into a shuddering mess. Viv could win, easy.

But Kendra wasn't about to admit it.

Viv smiled like she knew exactly what Kendra was thinking. "My four enticing smiles turning you on?"

"Uh…" Yes. God, yes.

Viv dragged her gaze down Kendra's body with an intensity that made Kendra shiver. Like now that Viv had finally allowed herself to look, she wasn't going to hold back. Or maybe she just really wanted to win.

"You never did tell me what I'm getting instead of a partridge in a pear tree," Viv said. "After the four enticing smiles and the three kisses and the two—"

"Is there a *reason* you started with day four instead of day five?"

"What's day five again?"

"You know perfectly well what it is." *Mind-blowing* might

be exaggerating, but… No, actually, mind-blowing was doable.

"Because there's no incentive to try to win if I don't like the prizes."

"That won't be an issue, since you'll be losing anyway. You'll be coming and coming and coming and losing it so bad that you won't even care that you're losing the compet—"

"Get in here," Viv said, slamming her book shut. "Get under the sheets."

As Kendra obeyed and wrestled Viv deeper under the covers, the last cheesy line of the song came to her, and she sang it into Viv's bellybutton. "And a love—"

"That tickles!" Viv shrieked, pushing her off, which brought Kendra even lower down her body. Lucky her.

She kept singing. "A loooove…that will last without end."

Chapter 6

Day 6

Kendra 1 : Viv 1

When Viv came home from the lab, Kendra was at the kitchen sink in yellow rubber gloves, wrist-deep in sudsy dishwater, scrubbing a casserole pan.

"Back so early?" Kendra teased.

It wasn't early. Kendra had already eaten dinner without her, which was pretty much what always happened on days she stayed home and Viv drove to work alone.

Viv circled around behind her and hugged her by the waist using only one arm, her body at an angle, like she wasn't planning on staying, and dropped a kiss on the back of her shoulder through her worn thermal shirt. "Missed you."

"You saw me this morning."

Viv kissed her again, this time on the back of her neck, lips touching skin.

The pan slipped out of Kendra's hands and banged into the stainless steel sink.

Kendra jumped.

Viv jumped worse. She laughed. "I thought *you* were supposed to be the romantic one. Now you're telling me you didn't miss me?"

"I missed you."

Viv hauled her close. "No you didn't. You were too busy

working to think about me at all."

Kendra sighed. She *had* been working. She'd finally made progress writing the grant proposal she'd been procrastinating on for weeks. Catching up on work was what vacations were for, right?

"Your shirt's wet," Viv said, like she'd only just now noticed. Like it didn't happen every single time Kendra did dishes, this big wet spot on her stomach.

Kendra shook her head. "That's what happens, babe. Things splash and water gets on the countertop."

"You don't have to lean on the wet countertop."

"And yet somehow I do."

"You're soaked." Viv tugged the hem away from Kendra's skin and wrung it out, but there wasn't enough moisture for it to have any effect. "Maybe when we replaced the countertops we should have had this one installed at an angle so it would drain into the sink."

"While our dishes would magically not slide away in a crash landing?"

Viv smiled against her neck. "Exactly. I'm sure we could engineer a solution."

Kendra loved that she could feel that smile on her skin. Viv moved her lips and sucked at her, and the only reason Kendra didn't drop any dishes this time was that her hands were empty.

Kendra gripped the edge of the sink. "Can you imagine trying to explain our innovative design requirements to the salesman?"

Viv let up on the kissing. Or whatever it was called when a woman mouthed at a sensitive area and then did it harder and more insistently when it became obvious she was making you lose your balance. Like she *wanted* you to lose your balance.

"That poor guy," Viv said. "Remember the look on his face when you told him the granite countertop he wanted to sell us wasn't granite?"

Come on, Viv. Less talking. More kissing.

"It's *not* granite," Kendra said, because she couldn't take her own advice and stop talking. "Look at it! Anyone can tell."

"Anyone who's taken your intro geology class."

"He works in a showroom filled with rocks. He should know the difference between granite and gneiss." And schist. And gabbro. And and and…

"If the company tells him all the pretty, polished slabs are called granite because it's too confusing for the customers to use unfamiliar words…"

"You're taking *his* side?"

"Aren't you the one who told me I didn't need to be precise when I measured my desk? That it was unromantic?"

"I'm also the one who told you I'm precise when it matters."

"This matters? Eh. It's just a rock." Viv snickered.

Kendra squirmed in her arms. "Get off me."

Keeping one arm firmly around Kendra's waist, Viv rubbed the smooth surface of their gneiss countertop, tracing the black and white bands that Kendra had taught her were key to its identification, silently communicating that she understood that yes, this *was* important to the geologist in the house.

"You did an excellent job of explaining metamorphism to him," Viv said. "I was a little turned on."

"You were not."

"I was. And I think the salesman might've been—"

"Stop! No. Yuck. Don't *say* things like that. Honestly, Viv. He thought I was harassing him. I feel bad."

"You weren't harassing him. You were…enthusiastic about your topic."

Kendra turned on the water to rinse her abandoned casserole pan.

Viv's hands snaked around Kendra's waist and fumbled for her belt.

"What are you doing?" Kendra asked, shutting off the water and immediately wanting to kick herself, because when Viv got daring, the best thing to do was let her do whatever she wanted. It was always worth it.

But Viv wasn't undoing Kendra's pants. Viv was…

Kendra glanced down. Her belt had already landed on the floor, but her pants remained buttoned and zipped. Viv wasn't touching her zipper at all. Instead, she was threading a handful of mistletoe through Kendra's now-empty belt loop. Trying to, anyway. She wasn't having much success doing it blind from behind.

"Where'd this come from?" The vine looked relatively fresh, so definitely not the same one they'd fought over the other day.

"When I checked in on my experiment this morning, Min-Jeong was in, picking up her students' exams, and she told me there was chocolate in Thor's office. When I stopped by to see if he had any left, he was in his doorway balancing on an out-of-date edition of the *Glossary of Infectious Diseases*, struggling to remove the mistletoe some kid had nailed there as a prank. Never noticed how short he is."

"So he handed the mistletoe over to you?"

Viv rested her chin on Kendra's shoulder so she could see what her fingers were doing. Didn't seem to help.

"I may have mentioned I'd be passing by the on-campus compostable waste disposal bin on my way out."

"Cute."

"Just trying to be helpful. You know me, always willing to step up and help out a colleague."

"Hmm. Is that what this is? You're helping me do the dishes?" Kendra removed her dishwashing gloves. If Viv got any more adorable, Kendra was not going to be able to concentrate on household chores. "Can't say I'm finding it very helpful."

"Did I say anything about dishes?"

"What, then?"

Still peering in vain over Kendra's shoulder, Viv grumbled something unintelligible and yanked on Kendra's belt loop.

Kendra smiled to herself. "Having trouble?"

"Is there a reason this mistletoe hates me?"

Kendra took Viv's hands and gently disengaged them from her waistband. "Can't decide if I should try to escape or if I should be patient and wait to see what your plan is."

"I think you have a pretty good sense of the plan already."

Viv turned her head and pressed a teasing kiss to the side of Kendra's neck in an obvious attempt to distract her while she freed her hands from Kendra's hold.

"You know what? I have a better plan."

Kendra spun around, and before Viv could react, Kendra had the mistletoe in her own hands and was tucking it into the waistband of Viv's jeans.

"Belt loops are too complicated," Kendra said, taking Viv by the shoulders and nudging her away from the sink as Viv gasped in indignation. Kendra backed her into the dining room toward the only wall that wasn't obstructed by furniture or artwork. "This way."

"Why?"

Kendra pressed Viv's back to the wall. "Why? Because I'm going to help you calculate your students' final grades."

"You're going to…" Viv tried to scowl at her, but she couldn't fool anyone with that cute face. "Unlikely."

Kendra cupped Viv's cheek, combed her fingers through Viv's hair, and trailed down her neck. "I knew you were smart."

Viv's lips parted. She wasn't breathing faster, but she wasn't arguing, either, so the reason her mouth was open wasn't speech-related. Maybe she was breathing a *little* faster.

"I *liked* my plan," Viv said. "You would have liked it, too."

Yeah, okay, fine. Talking. Kendra knew what Viv looked like when she was turned on, though, and this was unmistakably it. Her mouth kind of went slack and her forehead pinched and her eyes darkened and…

Kendra dropped to her knees less gracefully than she meant to.

Viv bit her lip in that way that meant she really, really wanted to say something, but she didn't think she should.

Kendra narrowed her eyes.

"Interesting technique," Viv commented.

Kendra shifted her weight and winced. This was why God invented beds. With comfy mattresses. And kneepads. And why it had been years since either she or Viv had attempted this.

"How do straight women do this?" Kendra said. "Because, one, this hurts my knees, and two, the angle is all wrong, so three, it's not my knees I'm most worried about, it's my neck, and four, I know the anatomy is different but is the angle really *that* different?"

"I don't think you're supposed to be talking while you do this."

Oh good, *now* Viv thought there was too much talking.

Kendra changed the way she was kneeling. Nope, didn't help. "I'm going to go with yes, the angle *is* different."

"Did I say *while* doing this? I meant *instead of* doing this."

"Maybe it's a height thing. If you were taller…" Kendra bent down and dropped a kiss on Viv's knee, the heavy denim cool against her lips.

"Or *you* were shorter…"

Viv rocked her hips. It was significantly more suggestive than Kendra had expected.

Kendra kissed a line up her inseam. "Does either one of us really know the answer?"

"No," Viv replied, wiggling like she was trying to maneuver Kendra into position.

Yeah, Kendra saw where this was going. She should reverse direction down Viv's thigh instead of higher where Viv was trying to lead her and see what happened.

"You don't know?" Kendra looked up. "Didn't you ever—"

"No."

"—with your boyfriends?"

"Absolutely not."

"Not even on a bed?"

"No," Viv said, sounding affronted. "Not vertically, not horizontally, not whatever."

"Not diagonally?"

"No, not diagonally. I don't even know what that means."

Kendra squinted up at her. "How did I not know this about you?"

"You never asked."

True. She knew Viv had dated guys when she was a teenager, but she'd always shied away from asking about the details. Some things were better left unsaid. Because she'd assumed there *were* details.

"You said you made out with some of them. I guess I thought—" Kendra stopped herself. Not going there. So it made perfect sense that her next words were, "You *never* did this with a guy?"

"I was saving myself for marriage."

After thousands of hours of conversation, Viv could still surprise her. Was that anywhere near the right number? Hmm. Say it was one hour of conversation per day. Three hundred sixty-five hours a year, bump it up to four hundred to make the math easier, four hundred times twenty-six years was...let's see, fudge the twenty-six to twenty-five...four quarters in a dollar...add two zeros...and end up with...ten thousand.

That didn't sound like much, not for twenty-six years. How could ten thousand—or even twenty thousand—hours feel like a lifetime?

Kendra opened Viv's zipper. "We should send you out on a research expedition to find out. See if the different anatomy makes a difference."

Viv pushed her hips forward, seeking Kendra's hand. "What kind of girlfriend are you, telling me to find a guy and report back like it's some scientific experiment?"

Kendra smiled into her denim-clad thigh. "A girlfriend with scientific curiosity?"

"You can picture it without collecting data."

"Ew. No visuals. Not while I've got my mouth on your mistletoe, thank you very much."

"I'm sorry, was your mouth actually touching me? I could have sworn I didn't feel a thing."

"Oh, you'll feel it." Kendra hooked her fingers under Viv's waistband in warning. The score was one and one, and Kendra was not going to let that stand. "I'm not scared of your good-girl reputation like your high school boyfriends were."

"They weren't scared. I was good at resisting."

"That does not surprise me in the least."

It pained her to think of a young, serious Viv doing her determined best to preserve her virtue, convinced that all the good behavior in the world wasn't enough to make her a good person unless she stopped boys from touching her. It was probably a blessing that Viv had never wanted them to touch her. All she'd wanted was for someone to like her. Kind, intelligent Viv, whose goodness should never have been questioned. Sweet, prickly Viv, who'd grown up to think it was okay that the viruses in her experiments saw more action than she did.

Wait, did viruses do that, or did they reproduce by...? Kendra shook her head. Never mind that.

"Is this really hurting your neck? We don't have to..." Viv started to push away from the wall.

Kendra gripped her hip bones and pushed her back. Viv's shoulders met the wall with a thud.

"We have to," Kendra said. "Now take these off."

Viv met her gaze for a long moment as if trying to decide whether Kendra was going to be complaining about neck pain for the rest of winter break if she let her go ahead with this.

"I'm already down here," Kendra said. "Getting up will hurt worse. So come on. Stop worrying about me and take your jeans off."

Viv laughed. "Stop. Your grumpy sex talk is turning me on." She smoothed a lock of hair off Kendra's forehead with a gentleness that made Kendra's throat tighten. "You'll make me come if you keep talking like that."

"I'm pretty sure it's going to take a bit more work than that."

"Mm." Viv toed off her shoes and curled her fingers around her waistband as Kendra helped her tug downward. The mistletoe tumbled to the floor, and Viv kicked it aside and stepped out of her jeans.

"Green underwear?" Kendra played with the elastic but made no move to pull it down. "How Christmas-y. Was this on purpose?"

"It was." Viv rocked forward a little, pushing into her hand.

It ought to have been tame—just Viv standing in her underwear—but kneeling and looking up at her, knowing Viv trusted her, was the best feeling in the world.

"Do I need to buy you Rudolph lingerie for your Christmas present?" Kendra asked.

"I think you meant to say you already have my Christmas present picked out."

"Yup. That *is* what I meant to say." It wasn't even a lie. They'd agreed years ago not to give each other Christmas gifts, but somehow they always ended up exchanging a couple of small, fun things they couldn't resist.

"And it had better not be Rudolph lingerie," Viv said.

Why? Because Viv had told her in no uncertain terms to never buy her lingerie? "Poinsettia."

"You'd better be lying."

"Yeah. Actually I found a set with gingerbread men performing questionable acts."

"You did not."

She didn't. "What's that supposed to mean? You think I don't know your size?"

Viv nudged her with a knee. "It means I already know what you got me, and I can't wait to see what kind of *it's-not-granite* you came up with this year."

"What? Why would you assume I'd give you a rock?"

"A rock wired as a desk lamp? A rock that's a decorative planter? A geode clock? A rock paperweight? Feel free to stop me anytime."

"You didn't like the desk lamp?" She really did try to think about the recipient, and what that person's interests were, when deciding on a gift. It was just that rocks were so fascinating, and so easy to turn into gift ideas, and viruses were so...*not*.

"I liked the desk lamp," Viv said.

"I wired it myself, you know."

"And I was impressed."

"Not everyone knows how to wire a—"

"I believe I may have shown you how impressed I was. With my mouth. And I wasn't using it to form words."

Oh yeah, she remembered. Viv had turned off the overhead lights and undressed by lamp glow. Followed by the not-talking part. That had been a fun Christmas.

"This year you're getting a really large decorative boulder for the front stoop," Kendra lied.

"Which you picked up during a field trip you were leading for your students?"

"Umm..." That did sound like something she'd do.

Perhaps Viv knew her a little too well.

Kendra pressed her mouth to the inside of Viv's bare thigh. They both fell silent. Yeah. Much better than talking.

Kendra worked her way up until she reached the crease of Viv's thigh and licked along the length of it, finding the spot where the femoral artery—Viv had taught her its name—pulsed just beneath the surface. God, she smelled good. Tasted good.

Viv reached for the wall behind her.

"Your knees okay?" Viv asked, her voice tight and her breathing a bit too fast.

"Absolutely."

Viv rocked her hips hesitantly, like she was holding back, afraid of knocking Kendra off-balance or hurting her.

Kendra dug into her with her thumbs to steady those hips, or maybe to steady herself. She felt Viv's pulse speed up, strong and even, under her tongue.

"If you want to stop…" Viv said.

And lose?

"Don't think so."

Viv wasn't going to deprive her of this. No way. Kendra loved doing this. Her knees weren't happy, but she wasn't *that* old. Jesus. She'd survive.

She pressed another kiss, openmouthed and insistent, to Viv's pulse point.

Viv was still holding up the wall. Her knuckles turned white.

Kendra pulled Viv's not-necessarily-Christmas underwear all the way down and licked into her wet heat.

Viv gasped. "Finally."

Finally? Was that all she had to say? Kendra slowed the movement of her tongue. *I'll show you* finally.

Viv groaned.

Kendra tightened her hold on Viv's thighs.

"Come on." Viv's voice was low and pleading. Breathless.

Kendra melted at the sound, helpless to do anything but chase Viv's pleasure and give her what she wanted, find her hardness and make it harder.

Viv groaned again, and Kendra's body thrummed with arousal. The more Viv panted, the more Viv slammed her ass into the wall and thrust forward, the more Kendra became so turned on that she had to concentrate on not losing her coordination.

"More," Viv whispered.

Kendra moaned into her, and Viv bucked her hips, hard, and came.

"My turn," Viv said after that, pulling Kendra shakily to her feet, and moments later the score was tied again.

Chapter 7

Day 7

KENDRA 2 : VIV 2

Kendra sent a text as she pulled into the lot behind Viv's building and parked in a prime spot reserved for someone with more seniority. Viv's assigned spot wasn't nearly as convenient, and there were only a few cars in the lot, so whatever.

Viv had gone in to check on her virus cultures, and, since they shared a single car, Kendra had dropped her off and taken the car to go grocery shopping.

Kendra sat in the car and waited for Viv to reply, searching in vain for a radio station that was not playing Christmas songs. One of these days she'd have to figure out how to stream music she actually liked.

Viv? I'm parked.

Still no reply.

Kendra sighed. When Viv was engrossed in the lab, it could be hard to get her attention. Even if her phone wasn't muted or forgotten in her office, she was completely capable of not hearing it at all.

Viv. I'm coming in.

Kendra cut off the radio mid-song, exited the car, and headed for Viv's office.

———

Viv was in the hallway, handbag over her shoulder and clearly on her way out, but she'd been waylaid by Thor—Theodore Cardini—her department chair. Viv acknowledged Kendra's arrival with a flicker of relief before turning her attention back to their conversation. Kendra leaned against the wall to wait.

"You're in town for the duration, right?" Thor was asking Viv. "Not visiting family?" Kendra had chosen a spot far enough away to give them the illusion of privacy, but she could hear every word, since Thor believed a thundering voice was key to holding students'—and faculty's—attention.

"No, I fly back to Argentina only in summer," Viv said. "That is to say, Northern Hemisphere summer. We do see Kendra's brother shortly before Christmas, but he's local."

"Good, because the development office has organized a New Year's Eve party for major donors," Thor said. "I want you there to tell the donors about the great things we're doing in our department. If you're available, of course."

Ugh. One of those work things that was phrased as a request to make it sound optional, but wasn't.

"Are you sure I'm the best choice for this?" Viv asked doubtfully. She had to know she was supposed to say yes, she'd be there, but hey, if she thought she could talk her way out of it, it was worth a shot.

Don't make it a question, babe. Tell *him you're not. Tell him you're terrible at coming up with amusing anecdotes.* Which was a lie, but if it worked…

"Neville is much better at this sort of thing," Viv told him. "*You* are much better at this sort of th—"

"But it's New Year's! Champagne. Dancing. No one wants to dance with a room full of boring old men like me and Neville, now do they?"

Viv's face went carefully blank.

No. No no no. Don't do this to her.

With her figure and her looks, Viv had always believed she had to ramp up the sexless brainiac vibe in order to be taken seriously as an intellectual equal. No amount of I'm-too-busy-being-academically-rigorous-to-even-think-about-flirting could make her less hot in Kendra's eyes, but Viv thought it helped at work, so who was Kendra to try to stop her? Even when untouchable in public became so ingrained she sometimes became untouchable in private, too, and hurt something deep in both their souls.

"Neville's not old," Viv said. "Neither are you."

"So diplomatic. That's why you're the perfect choice."

"Because I can discuss HIV research diplomatically? Or because I'm a respected expert in my field?"

There was a dangerous edge to her voice, but Thor laughed, like he thought Viv was joking.

"Also," Viv said, "I don't dance."

"Don't be so modest. You Latinas are born with rhythm."

Uh-oh.

Viv and Kendra exchanged a look.

Kendra's look said, *That sensitivity training they force us all to sit through really works, doesn't it?*

Viv's look said, *Kendra, don't kill him.*

Hmm. Perhaps Kendra's look had not said quite what she thought it had.

Viv's look also said, *I'll handle this. Not you.*

Kendra nodded her encouragement.

Viv crossed her arms and straightened her shoulders and turned back to Thor. "*If* I attend, I will *not* be dancing."

Thor's smile faltered. "Well, hey, I understand. Not in your job description, I guess."

"I need to get going," Viv said, because she really *was* diplomatic. "Shall we discuss this later? My ride is here."

"Yes. Sure. I'll call you. But Viv. Listen. The party will be fun. You'll have a great time."

"Hmm," Viv answered noncommittally.

Ugh. Sounded like Viv might not get out of this one.

"Come on, Kendra." Viv headed her direction and Kendra pushed away from the wall to join her. "Let's go before you're caught parked in someone else's space."

"How did you—"

"I know you."

Which felt so wonderful that Kendra almost reached for her hand.

She didn't, though, because Thor was watching, and she didn't want to see Viv flinch.

———

"It's okay to be both sexy and smart," Kendra told Viv through the partially closed bathroom door, waiting in bed for Viv to finish brushing her teeth. If their run-in with her colleague had reminded Viv of all the reasons she had to shut down… "It doesn't have to be one or the other."

"I know," Viv said.

"Because you know it's day seven, and—"

"Worried?"

Viv emerged from the bathroom wearing not the ever-present pajamas but a negligee Kendra had almost forgotten about. The skirt part was solid black silk that draped from an empire waist to her knees, while the upper panel was black lace that made it impossible not to notice the exact color of her nipples.

Kendra blinked. Why had Viv decided to keep this negligee all these years rather than donate it to Goodwill? And how did it still fit?

She realized with a pang that she couldn't remember the first time she'd seen Viv wear this thing, or when she'd stopped, or why.

"This is unlike you, Viv."

Except it was. It *was* like her. She could shy away and then an hour later do *this*.

"You *should* be worried," Viv said. "You should be worried that you're going to lose."

"No way."

"Yes way," Viv said, neglecting to turn off the lights before she padded toward the bed, all slinky without hardly trying.

Kendra shook her head, impressed. "If you're using this to gain an edge in the competition, it won't work."

"It won't?" Viv said, sliding under the covers.

The score was two and two, so no, it *wasn't* going to work. Kendra had a plan. She was going to make Viv come and then she was going to make sure she didn't come herself. She wasn't the type of person who forgot her plan and turned stupid at the sight of the woman she loved wearing lace that was…what was the word? Uh…yeah. Extremely see-through.

"I like you in your normal clothes," Kendra muttered.

"That lace looks itchy."

Viv shrugged. Kendra did *not* notice how her breasts moved up and down.

"Won't you be cold in that?"

Viv scooted closer to Kendra's side of the bed. "Oh, I think I can come up with a way to heat up."

"Perfect," Kendra grumbled, sliding down her pillow in surrender and pushing the sheets off her chest, suddenly much too warm. "I thought the six cheesy come-ons were supposed to be yesterday."

Viv encroached even more until she was completely on Kendra's side of the bed. Together, in silent agreement, they tugged off Kendra's sleep shirt and underwear. Viv crawled on top of her as Kendra lay on her back, tugging Viv into place.

Viv braced herself on her forearms. "Cold?" she asked, grinning down at her.

"If I say yes, will you do this all night?"

"What, lie on top of you?"

Kendra nodded.

"And sleep?"

"Yeah," Kendra said, because resisting the more energetic option was the plan. Besides, sleeping like this did sound nice.

"Of course," Viv said. "But first I have something I have to do." She slid up Kendra's body, making as much contact as possible. "Win."

"I don't think so."

"You're going to beg me to win," Viv promised, the challenge in her voice doing nothing to conceal her affection. She rolled off of her and slid her palm, firm and sure, up Kendra's inner thigh.

Kendra arched. "I'm not..." Viv kept going, and she arched even higher, until her spine felt like it might cramp. "I'm not begging."

"Not yet."

Viv was...holding her. Cradling her. At the juncture of her thighs.

If only Kendra could relax, she'd probably admit it was pleasant.

Soothing.

Good.

She could lie here, enjoying Viv's easygoing seduction, no expectations, no pressure, and just be, just feel, just sink into how nice it felt, maybe eventually even be in danger of dozing off if it weren't so...

Maddening.

What was Viv doing? It felt good, of course it felt good, and she wouldn't mind falling asleep with Viv's hand between her legs—and waking up a little before midnight, just in time to score a point against Viv—but it wasn't *enough*. It made her *want*. It made her squirm.

She needed Viv to *do* something. Anything.

Kendra's knees slid apart. She couldn't help it.

Viv moved her hand, just a little.

More. Babe. Please.

Viv stroked down her inner thigh. And let go.

Kendra squeezed her legs together and clenched her pillow in frustration.

"Viv."

"You're right. That doesn't sound like begging at all."

"You..."

Viv smiled as she lowered her head. Kendra tightened in anticipation, watching her moisten her lips, riveted by the slight movement of Viv's throat as she swallowed.

Closer…and closer…and closer…

Viv sucked her nipple into her mouth. It hardened instantly.

"Fuck. Viv."

Viv licked sweetly at her like she was trying to make her harder, like that might even be possible. Arousal coiled and uncoiled inside her, pulsing with the rhythm of Viv's tongue.

Viv pulled off her nipple, leaving it wet. Viv stared at what she'd done and her breath hitched.

Kendra reached up and tucked Viv's hair behind her ears, lingering to trace her eyebrows, her cheekbones, her jaw. "You're so…" *Beautiful. Impossible. Perfect.*

Viv touched her tongue to the wetness she'd left, barely moving, but utterly, completely focused.

Kendra's ribs moved up and down. She might have been panting.

She was supposed to resist. She *needed* to resist. That was the plan. She *wanted* to be flushed and squirming and not…*not*…losing control. She wanted Viv so preoccupied that she wouldn't notice Kendra was running out the clock.

So if Viv wanted to take her time, that was a good thing.

Really.

A good thing.

A very good thing.

Kendra moaned in frustration. If Viv's touch got any better, it was all going to be over.

Viv made a satisfied sound and closed her lips on her.

"*Viv.*" Her voice sounded oddly strangled.

Viv rubbed against her side, warm and familiar, then swung a leg over her thighs to straddle her. Kendra stretched up to kiss her, and Viv cradled the back of her head, supporting her, and kissed her back.

Once again Kendra's legs slid apart, but this time, with Viv on top of her, her knees pushed at Viv's thighs until Viv had to spread her own legs to accommodate her.

Kendra gripped Viv's ass, pulling her close, anchoring herself against the rush of vertigo as Viv rolled off her again, never breaking the kiss.

"Love you," Viv said against her mouth. And pressed between her legs. Almost inside her, but not quite.

Kendra's thighs trembled. The warmth and the gentle pressure of her hand, her mouth, her body—her love—made her ache.

The plan was in trouble. The only way to salvage it would be to turn this around and make Viv come first. She'd need to not let Viv make her come, and not let her and not let her and not let her, and then it would be midnight and *then* she could come. After.

Viv kissed the base of her throat.

Kendra's inner muscles clenched as if Viv was already inside her.

But Viv wasn't inside her. She was circling, gliding in slick.

"Viv. For God's sake."

Viv continued to circle, slow and deliberate.

Kendra was going to kill her.

After Viv gave her what she wanted.

No. She wasn't supposed to let Viv give her what she wanted.

No. Fuck the challenge. She needed Viv to—

"It's early," Viv said. "We have time." She paused. "Before time runs out."

Kendra lifted her head in disbelief, glared, and flopped

back onto the pillow. "You're thinking about the competition right now?"

"And you're not?"

Yes, fine, she was.

She wished she wasn't.

"If you don't touch me where I need you sometime this century," Kendra said, recklessly disregarding her plan because she couldn't remember why she'd come up with it, "you won't win."

"Don't worry, I'll make you come."

"I'm not *worried*, I'm…God, I can't think like this, just…oh." Kendra's hips thrust hard. She could make Viv slip. She could show her where she wanted her.

As if Viv didn't know.

Viv didn't slip.

Kendra thrust again, harder. She needed Viv to move, goddammit. Frustration whipped her head left and right, and somewhere in the midst of it, she caught a glimpse of the bedside clock.

"Is that an eleven?" she said, turning to get a better look, but Viv shifted and obstructed her view.

"What, on the clock? No."

"What time is it, then?"

Viv turned her away from the clock and slid home. She curled her fingers inside her, and it was like she was still holding her, still cradling her.

Kendra shuddered and let her. "Oh. My. *God.*"

"Five minutes till midnight," Viv whispered.

"What?"

Kendra moaned. The scheming little shit had stolen her idea. Made Kendra believe her strategy was to wear that see-through negligee while she snuck her real plan right past her.

Sabotaged her. And now they were out of time. Correction: *Kendra* was out of time. Viv was about to squeak out a point right before midnight, and Kendra didn't think she had it in her to stop it.

"You did this on purpose."

She should have made Viv come first. She should have been thinking more clearly.

"Mm?" Viv moved slowly in and out.

Viv was so good at this.

So.

Good.

She'd been good when they first met, but years of experience had made her great. She knew exactly how to make Kendra lose her mind.

Viv pushed into her harder, forcing an embarrassing sound from Kendra's lungs.

"You totally…did…this…on…purpose."

"Was I supposed to put my hand here by accident?" Viv asked mildly.

"You know what I mean."

"Mm." Viv adjusted her angle.

Kendra trembled helplessly as the energy of impending orgasm took over and rose up her spine. Her heels dug into the mattress and her hips lifted. The backs of her legs were on the verge of cramping and she was so close, so close, so…so…so…*God…Viv…I love you…*

She sobbed as her hips arched impossibly higher, and then she lost it, crying out in relief.

———

"Midnight," Viv said. "How about that. I'm ahead by one

point."

Kendra laughed up at the ceiling and tucked Viv more securely against her shoulder, their bodies tangled together on the bed.

"I let you win," Kendra said.

"Yeah, no. You didn't."

No, she hadn't, but she was too relaxed and blissed out to care. "You can make it up to me later."

"Why would I want to do that?" Viv said.

"Because it's more challenging when the score is tied."

"Seems to me it's more challenging for *you* the way the score is right now."

"You might be right," Kendra said, stroking the fine hairs on Viv's forearm in the dark. "But I wouldn't want to deprive you of a challenge."

"I don't feel deprived."

"You're enjoying this."

Viv twined her leg around Kendra's. "Of course not. I don't enjoy winning at your expense."

"Oh, you totally do. You totally, totally, totally—"

Viv kissed her, which did a good job of shutting her up.

She was pretty sure Viv was smiling.

Chapter 8

Day 8

KENDRA 2 : VIV 3

"Don't want to be late," Kendra said, barging into their bedroom with Viv's morning coffee. "Oh good. You're up."

"What shoes are you wearing?" Viv asked, barefoot in jeans as she pulled her rattiest sweatshirt on over her head. They were driving out to a Christmas tree farm this morning with Kendra's brother and his kids to saw down a couple trees, and tree sap might be involved.

"My field boots."

"Do you think it'll be muddy?" Viv sipped the coffee Kendra handed her and opened a dresser drawer to pick out a pair of warm socks. "My hiking boots hurt my feet. I'd rather wear my sneakers."

"Then wear your sneakers," Kendra said, relieving her of the socks to take her hand and stroke her knuckles. "It's not exactly wilderness out there."

"It's the same place we went last year, though, right? That place was in the mountains. It was steep."

"I'll save you if you slide down the mountain in shoes with no tread."

"In that case, I might have to slip on purpose." Viv pulled her in, her gaze lowered to Kendra's lips, her voice turning sultry and morning-rough. "I understand pine needles on the ground can be quite hazardous."

Kendra found her mouth, and Viv's coffee mug barely made it safely to the top of the dresser as she met her kiss. Kendra crowded into Viv's space, unwilling to let her go, and Viv melted into her, tasting of coffee and peppermint and home.

"Someone should post a warning by the trees," Viv murmured when she came up for air. "Wouldn't be America without a safety warning."

She sought Kendra's mouth again, and Kendra curled a hand around Viv's neck and threaded her fingers through her bed head, wanting her to feel how precious she was to her.

She was very tempted to pull Viv back into the bed she'd just gotten out of, but she also didn't want to have to lie to her brother about why they were late.

"Shoes," Kendra said, finally ending their kiss.

Viv picked up the socks that Kendra had apparently dropped on the floor. "You'd really try to catch me if I slipped?"

"Yup. We'd probably both end up on the ground, hurt, though."

Viv sat on the bed to pull on her socks and flashed a mischievous smile. "Or winning day eight."

"Only one of us is winning day eight," Kendra said. "I'm going to get you back for last night."

"Doubtful."

"You'll see."

————

It took over two hours of traipsing up and down the rows of Fraser firs before they found a tree Kendra's nieces could agree on. Every tree they saw was too short, according to Zima, or too tall, according to their father, or had a weird gap between its branches, according to Jill.

Deciding on Kendra's and Viv's Christmas tree was easy in comparison—Viv picked it out, and Kendra said *fine with me*, and Zima and Jill gave Kendra puzzled looks, like didn't she *care*, and that was it.

Well, not completely it. They still had to return to the farm's entrance to borrow a bow saw. Also, while Harlan, Kendra's brother, talked to one of Santa's helpers about the saw, Viv quietly asked another employee for a measuring pole.

"All the ten-footers are taken," the guy apologized. "The fifteen-foot pole can be awkward, but you're welcome to try it."

"No problem," Viv said. "We'll take it."

"We will?" Kendra lifted one from the ground and set it back down. It was steel with slashes of orange paint marking the number of feet, and *awkward* was right. Planting it upright next to their tree without bashing anyone in the head with it might be a challenge.

"We will," Viv said. "Their tree needs to fit inside their house."

"We don't need a measuring pole for that," Kendra protested, just to be contrary, even though Viv was right to insist. "I'll stand next to the tree, and the girls can decide who's taller, me or the tree. Right, girls?"

Zima, the younger one, was enthusiastic, but Jill wrinkled her forehead and looked back and forth between Kendra and Viv, like maybe Viv would tell her if Aunt Kendra was joking. "What if it's a lot taller than you?"

"Well, that was only step one, obviously," Kendra explained. "Step two is, you imagine me standing in your living room, and imagine your ceiling, and there you go."

Viv made a face. "That sounds accurate."

"It'll be fun," Kendra said.

"I'll certainly be measuring *our* tree with the pole," Viv said.

"I want to measure with Aunt Viv," Jill said.

"Me too!" said Zima.

"Dad," Jill said. "How high is our ceiling?"

"Eight feet," Harlan said.

Traitors.

Kendra sighed and nodded to Harlan. He picked up one end, and together the two of them carried the pole up the hill, Viv alongside them with the bow saw and the girls running ahead.

Claiming the first tree took quite a bit more walking, several minutes of arguing between Jill and Zima over who got to use the saw, and a little adult help when it turned out the sawing was more challenging than they'd thought.

The second tree was quicker. Viv sawed, and Kendra held the tree stable. Kendra might have also surreptitiously ogled her while Viv lay on her side under the lowest branches going at the trunk, grunting with effort. That part had certainly gotten her into the Christmas spirit.

Viv would tell her that dragging their fragrant firs to the parking lot and tying them to the roofs of their vehicles was what was supposed to get her into the Christmas spirit.

And maybe it was both those things.

———

That night, after Viv had seen God or whatever those gasps had been about that turned Kendra on like crazy,

Kendra had slumped between her legs and contemplated her strategy while Viv caught her breath.

She'd learned her lesson the day before, and this time, she'd made sure Viv came first. So now what? Idea number one: she could repeat the previous night's disaster and let Viv touch her but try to not let it go too far. She wasn't good at resisting her, though, so…no. Idea number two: distract her. But with what? Um…drawing a blank on that one. Idea number three: avoid her. Which had to be against the rules, even though they'd never discussed it. No, she had to give Viv a chance. Although…sleeping wasn't really avoiding, was it? Sleeping might happen naturally. They were in bed, after all. That's what beds were *for*.

Kendra slowly, carefully, moved away and settled on her own pillow. Cutting their tree and securing it in the stand and decorating it had been exhausting. Definitely. Truly, utterly, thoroughly exhausting. Viv might believe that, right?

Kendra sank deeper into her pillow.

"Kendra?" Viv reached over in the dark and found her shoulder. "Ready?"

Kendra kept her eyes closed and didn't respond.

"Kendra?" The sheets rustled and the mattress dipped as Viv moved. Kendra could sense her looming over her, likely propped on one elbow. "You asleep?"

Kendra tried not to laugh. She couldn't believe she was cheating.

She couldn't believe she was getting away with it.

"You'd better not be faking," Viv whispered.

Kendra slowed her breathing and made her face relax.

Viv flopped onto her side of the bed and the mattress bounced again. "Sleep well, my little faking faker. Rest up for what's coming tomorrow, because you're going to need it."

Wait. Did that mean Viv believed her? Or didn't believe her? The *faking faker* thing might just be her being annoyed at being thwarted. Or it might mean Viv knew she was awake. Kendra took a slow breath, afraid to breathe at all.

"And when I say *tomorrow*, I mean *today*. So congratulations. You've slept past midnight and tied the score."

Really? Already? Kendra's eyes flew open to check the time.

"Ah ha!" Viv cried. "I knew it."

Kendra hid her face in her pillow and groaned. "It's not midnight, is it? You lied."

"It's only eleven."

"Crap."

"Plenty of time for me to even the score."

"The score *was* even. Now you're going to be ahead again."

"Probably."

Kendra sighed. Crap. At least losing at Viv's hands would feel good. If she could stop thinking about the score, what Viv was about to do to her would feel really, really, *really* good.

Chapter 9

Day 9

KENDRA 3 : VIV 4

Kendra knocked on Viv's open office door—Rudolph was still there, a red nose in the dark—and entered without waiting for an answer. "Ready to go?"

"Already shut down my computer." Viv extracted her handbag from her desk drawer and plopped it on top of her desk and then stuffed some work into her briefcase to take home.

Kendra was wearing her wool coat. She'd already had to brave the evening chill to walk from her own building to Viv's, and she'd have to do it again to get to their reserved parking spot in the faculty lot to drive home, but now that she was indoors the coat was hanging open, unzipped over her professorial turtleneck and jacket. She dropped her messenger bag on the floor and pushed the heavy fabric of the coat out of the way to wrap her arms around Viv from behind.

"I've been thinking about our lyrics," Kendra said into Viv's neck, pressing into her body heat.

"Yeah?"

She nuzzled into her hair. "Nine suggestive whispers."

Viv squirmed in her arms and turned around. She put her hands on Kendra's chest and tried to push her away while simultaneously caressing Kendra's breasts in a manner that did *not* mean *go away*. "Eight dirty looks."

That was Viv, the queen of mixed messages.

Kendra pulled her closer. "Seven braless outings."

"You are out of your mind."

"Too many syllables," Kendra said.

"What?"

"'You are out of your mind' is too many syllables for the song."

"It wasn't for the song."

Footsteps sounded in the hall, and Kendra remembered she hadn't pulled the door all the way shut when she'd come in. Viv escaped her hold. The footsteps came closer. Kendra reached out and smoothed Viv's hair into place, careful to maintain some space between their bodies while she listened for the person to stop and unlock one of the many doors along the way.

"Think they'll notice your light's on?" Kendra murmured.

Viv eyed the partly open door and nodded mutely. There was nothing like a row of dark, shut offices to make the one occupied one irresistible to anyone who passed.

Kendra glanced down at herself. Her coat was slipping off and the jacket underneath it was off-center and bunched in ways she never would have managed on her own. She tugged the incriminating evidence back into place and instantly regretted it, because those wrinkles had been a victory.

She must have made a sound because Viv shook her head sharply, a silent warning that time was up.

A tall, lanky, bearded guy stuck his head in the doorway, clasping the molding and swinging from one long arm like a big kid in a playground. "Doctor Ortiz! You're coming tomorrow, right? To our Christmas Eve party?"

Had to be one of Viv's postdocs. They were the only ones who stuck around during winter break, too paranoid about their careers to leave the lab for a few days.

Viv patted the back of her hair nervously even though Kendra had done a decent job fixing it. "I…uh…" She sounded like she was trying to catch her breath.

"Did Antoine remember to send you an invite?" The guy leaned farther into the office. "He's hosting 'cause he has the biggest place. Five housemates, can you believe that shit?"

Kendra tried very hard to read the titles on Viv's bookshelf to avoid making eye contact with Viv, because she was not at all sure it wouldn't be obvious that all she could think about was jumping the young man's professor.

"I received the invitation," Viv said. "Wouldn't miss it."

"You need the address?"

"It was in the invitation, I believe. Should I bring anything?"

"Your party attitude. And your distinguished colleague here."

Kendra looked over, surprised, and he winked.

"My…" Viv cleared her throat. "Jonah, have you met—"

"No worries, Doctor Ortiz. We all know Doctor Davis."

They did? Kendra was sure she'd never set eyes on this man in her life, but she supposed she did stop by Viv's lab most evenings for their drive home, and students did gossip among themselves.

"Good," Viv said, sounding a bit surprised herself. "So we'll see you at the party."

"Excellent! See you tomorrow." He swung again from the doorframe, this time in reverse, and left as abruptly as he'd arrived.

Viv shrugged into her coat. "I don't know what makes him think I have a party attitude."

Kendra picked up her own bag off the floor. "I don't know what makes you think you don't."

"I thought you'd lived with me long enough to notice I'm awful at—"

"You know how to be fun," Kendra said. "Maybe not drunken karaoke-singing fun, but—"

"Tell me that is not what we're going to be doing at this party."

"Guess we'll find out."

"Promise me you will not sing about seven braless outings."

"Hmm." Kendra smiled. Viv knew she'd never do it because she'd never embarrass her, but she couldn't resist. "What do I get if I promise?"

"You get to live."

"No, really. I think I should get something. I should get... Ooh! I know. I should get a bonus attempt. Tonight. You on the bed, me—"

"You do not get a bonus attempt. That is not in the rules." Viv jingled her keys in Kendra's direction, shooing her out the door so she could follow her out and lock up.

"Then I at least get to go first tonight. I get the first attempt."

"So you can pretend you're winning for five minutes before I get my turn to blow your mind?"

Kendra swallowed hard. "You'll be nonfunctional for longer than five minutes."

Viv shoved her keys into her coat pocket. "We'll have to see about that, won't we?"

Chapter 10

Day 10

KENDRA 3 : VIV 4 (12:01 a.m.) ... KENDRA 4 : VIV 4 (now)

Kendra sat on their living room sofa, shoes off, feet up, reading *Contributions to Mineralogy and Petrology* on her tablet while she waited for Viv to finish getting dressed. She'd found an interesting paper written by someone she'd met at a conference in Prague. She'd kind of rather stay home reading than drag her body off the sofa and stay out late. Not because she was getting old, but because she enjoyed reading, and because there was never enough time in the day to keep up with what was being published in her field.

When she heard Viv come down the stairs from the bedroom and looked up from her journal, though, the party became more interesting. Viv was wearing a boat-neck sheath dress that ended just below her knees, showing off her killer calves and her beloved, adorable, but defiantly unfashionable ankle boots. Watching Viv in that outfit versus getting to the end of this scientific paper? Easy answer.

The journal fell to her lap. "You look nice." Understatement.

Viv smoothed her hands over her hips and fussed unnecessarily with her hemline, tugging at it as if it wasn't already straight, turning to show off how the skirt hugged her ass, looking over her shoulder to watch Kendra's reaction.

Like she didn't know Kendra would never look away.

"Really," Kendra said.

Viv remembered herself—or pretended to—and huffed. "My eyes are up here." She extended two fingers in a V shape and pointed to herself.

"Are they," Kendra said in the bored, uninterested tone of voice she reserved for pointless faculty meetings. She let her gaze roam deliberately up and down Viv's body. "I don't care."

"So confident." Viv's voice softened. Her eyes darkened, and her lips parted like she was thinking about kissing her. "But you're not going to win."

"You sure about that?" Kendra swung her legs off the sofa, slipped on her shoes, retrieved her bag from the floor, and stalked over to Viv.

"One attempt per day," Viv reminded her. "You already had your chance."

She'd won it, too, getting Viv hot and bothered in the morning right before Viv needed to rush out the door to check on her lab and see what her favorite cells and viruses were up to today. Excellent timing, if she did say so herself.

Viv turned to the closet by the front door for their coats and handed over Kendra's. Instead of putting it on, Kendra threw the coat over her arm so she could take advantage of Viv's back being turned and hover. And run her fingers under Viv's neckline to make sure her bra straps were tucked securely underneath. Or maybe other reasons.

"Enjoy the score being tied while you can," Viv said, relaxing into her touch. Apparently she thought she'd have time to win her own point tonight.

Guess that meant they'd be leaving the party early, if Viv had her way. Kendra would just have to distract her.

"I am." She dropped a kiss on Viv's cheek. "Let's go."

———

When they arrived at the old row house a few blocks from campus, the party was already in full swing, Christmas music cranked to full volume, jingle bells hanging from the door knocker, colored lights strung around the windows. Viv was mobbed the minute the two of them stepped inside.

Kendra surveyed the room as Viv was dragged away by her students to talk shop. The only person she recognized, aside from the enthusiastic Jonah from the previous evening, was a professor in Viv's department whom she'd talked to a few times at department functions. Min-Jeong was just saying goodbye to two of her own fans, so after Kendra found the bedroom where guests' coats were thrown on the bed and added their own, she snagged a ginger ale and joined her at the dessert table.

Across the living room, students hovered around Viv, eager to be part of her circle, basking in her attention, no doubt spouting witty, intelligent comments in the hope of impressing her. Viv looked comfortable with them. Happy. Kendra's heart melted a little, seeing her like that.

Eventually, Viv freed herself and joined them.

"Hi, Min-Jeong," Viv said, nodding to them both and ignoring the gingerbread cookies Kendra hadn't been able to resist.

"Viviana. You look not yourself."

"I…" Viv looked confused, like she couldn't figure out which of the two of them had mistranslated.

"You look relaxed," Min-Jeong clarified.

Viv's smile reappeared. "Do I?" She shrugged. "I

suppose being on winter break could explain that."

"I didn't think you paid much attention to such things," said Min-Jeong. "The university informs us it is time for break, but who listens? Not you, I think. You work hard."

"Doctor Davis," interrupted one of Kendra's former students, appearing out of nowhere and waving one of those goofy reindeer antler headbands. "You look like you're in need of festive headgear."

Kendra's momentary delight at encountering a former student evaporated. What was the obsession with antlers this year?

"I can see you haven't heard that Doctor Davis is a grinch," Viv said, coming to Kendra's rescue.

"They're geologic," the student explained to them both. "Antler fossils are a thing."

"They're plush," Kendra countered.

"They *could* be fossils," the student said. "But give me a couple of those cream cheese brownies with the crushed peppermint on top and I'll find someone else who wants them."

"Deal."

The student ran off to find another victim and Kendra downed another cookie. Viv slung an arm over Kendra's shoulder, and Kendra's eyes widened at the public gesture.

"Having a good time?" Kendra asked.

"Mm." Viv took Kendra's red Solo cup from her and downed the last swallow of ginger ale without asking. "You know what this party really needs?"

"Better music?" Kendra reclaimed her cup and swirled the remains of her ice cubes, contemplating whether to have them now or wait until they melted more.

"What this party needs," Viv said, "is ten lords a-leaping."

Kendra's cup froze on the way to her mouth.

Viv didn't mean *at the student party*. No way. There was *no way*. They didn't even touch in front of the students. No hand on a shoulder, no kisses, no nothing.

Kendra tilted her head back and finished the dregs of her ginger-flavored meltwater. She lowered her cup, the ice sliding noisily back down, and stole a glance at Min-Jeong. "No leaping," she said. "This music is too boring to dance to."

Viv shrugged. "The students like it."

"And even they won't dance to it."

"Is that what *a-leaping* means? Dancing?" Viv's voice was absolutely neutral.

It made Kendra's competitive streak stir.

I'm trying to help here. But if you don't want me to...

Kendra caught an ice cube in her mouth and sucked on it. "What do you think it means?"

Answer. I dare you.

"Well. You know." Viv stayed completely bland. "Leaping."

"Jumping," Min-Jeong offered, as if Kendra were one of their foreign students who didn't have a firm grasp of English vocabulary.

"Jumping," Kendra repeated, sucking on her ice a little harder and giving Viv a pointed look as she rolled it around in her mouth to speak. "Not sure I approve of students jumping each other in public."

Viv coughed. "Not that kind of jumping. The kind where they climb on lab tables and leap off, throwing their arms wide and smacking the ceiling and wondering how the ceiling came to be so low. And that's before they start drinking."

Min-Jeong shook her head as if she too had witnessed the same thing in her own lab. She turned to the dessert table and selected a star-shaped sugar cookie. "Lords a-leaping." She reached for the stack of festive red and green napkins and took several. "It must mean dancing." She bit off a triangular point of her cookie and dabbed at her lips with a napkin. "What else?"

"Yeah." Kendra angled away from Min-Jeong to wink at Viv. "What else?"

Chapter 11

Day 11

KENDRA 4 : VIV 4 (12:01 a.m.) ... KENDRA 4 : VIV 5 (now)

"For someone who claims to want to win, you're not winning much," Viv teased Kendra as Christmas Day dwindled to a close.

They were sitting together on the living room sofa in the dark, breathing in the scent of their Fraser fir, watching its shadowy shape and its twinkling multicolored lights. The silk scarf printed with a partridge in a pear tree—Kendra's gift to Viv—lay abandoned on the floor with their shoes and half their clothing. Kendra had her arm over the back of the sofa and around Viv, and Viv rested her head on Kendra's shoulder, eyes closed, hair a wreck, her breathing synchronized with the rhythm of the rise and fall of Kendra's chest as she lazily attempted to button Kendra's open shirt.

Kendra should have known better. She'd let Viv get the upper hand, and now she was drifting off and she had no idea what time it was, and that was probably a bad move, considering what happened the last time she'd lost track. She had time, though, didn't she? To win a point? A few hours, at least.

Kendra ordered herself to stay awake, but her body wouldn't listen.

As she hovered on the edge of dropping off to sleep,

she thought she heard Viv say, "I made you come so hard you passed out again, huh?" Viv laughed quietly to herself. "That was too easy."

Viv thought she was winning? Kendra was going to get her for this. As soon as she had the energy to open her eyes.

"I won't wake you," the sneaky thing whispered, snuggling closer.

Shit. She couldn't...open...her...eyes.

Viv's lips brushed across her forehead. "I love you."

And then she was smoothing Kendra's hair until the soothing rhythm relaxed Kendra into unconsciousness.

Chapter 12

Day 12

KENDRA 4 : VIV 5

"Are you still working?" Viv asked, wandering into the dining room where Kendra had her papers spread out all over the big oval table.

Kendra leaned her elbows on the table and rubbed her forehead, pressing her thumbs into the tight muscles above her eyes. "I should quit for the day. I've been planning my lectures for next semester for...n, where n is a large number of hours."

Viv stood beside her chair and pulled Kendra to her chest. "Where n plus one is the number of hours after which your head explodes?"

Kendra tucked into her, burrowing her face in Viv's breasts, and laughed. "Yeah. Let's hope not."

Viv palmed the back of her head and gently stroked the base of her skull. "Why don't we play it safe and call it a night."

Kendra nuzzled her and nodded. "You wearing that see-through thing again? Because you're not tricking me like that anymore."

"Tricking you?" Viv asked innocently.

"Wear it if you want. Or the pajamas. Or nothing, I don't care." She gave Viv a squeeze before reluctantly releasing her.

"Tonight's day twelve. My last chance to win. And I'm going to."

"I'm ahead by one point," Viv reminded her with a smile. "The best you can hope for is a tie."

"I'm okay with a tie."

"I'm not."

"So competitive," Kendra said fondly, taking Viv's hand and bringing it to her mouth to kiss the faded scars. "And so going to lose." Keeping hold of her hand, she rose from her chair to lead her to the bedroom. "Get ready to have your mind blown."

Viv followed along and closed the bedroom door behind them. "I thought the blowing of the mind was reserved for day five."

"Aw, you remembered our lyrics," Kendra said, taking hold of the hem of Viv's sweater. "Now let's get these clothes off."

Viv captured her hands to stop her. "You first."

She should have known Viv would make this difficult.

"I'll undress as soon as you do."

"Or first," Viv suggested, kissing the base of her neck, bringing the scent of cinnamon and curry powder which clung to her hair from the candied nuts she'd baked earlier in the day.

"This is silly."

"It's strategic. You can't win unless you get me naked."

Kendra abandoned her attempt on her sweater and slid her hands underneath it and around her waist. "You think I have to get you naked to make you come? Please. Don't insult me."

Viv shivered. "Prove it."

"Like you don't remember all the times I've done it?"

Kendra scoffed.

She nudged Viv onto the bed and Viv let her, and before long Viv was lying on her back with a dazed look in her eyes and close to coming apart. Zipper open, clothes on, rocking into Kendra's hand.

Doing this to someone she loved was a completely different experience than her vague memories of doing it to someone she barely knew. Back when Kendra was dating, she'd focused a lot on her technique, learning each new person's body and trying to get it right.

With Viv, though, it wasn't about figuring out what Viv liked. It wasn't even really about concentrating on getting Viv off. She knew that part would happen.

With Viv, she could relax into feeling, and touching, and breathing into the love that burned from her core and bubbled up in her heart until it spilled over into their kisses and flowed out through her hands to join the love that flowed through Viv's hands just as much. Filled her, until it became the only thing that mattered.

Nothing they did with their bodies meant anything without that light. That joy. That connection, not with Viv's body, but with her essence. Her soul. Her being.

She loved her whether they did the *oh-my-God-now-now-now-you-talented-evil-genius-oh-God-yes* stuff or not. But she wouldn't trade the past eleven days for anything.

All of it was part of who she was. Who they both were.

She loved talking together. She loved hearing her laugh.

She loved the way Viv was now, flushed and desperate and writhing. Fighting it. Wanting it. Wanting her.

Kendra kissed the spot right over her heart, and Viv's breathing changed from ragged to frantic.

"Babe," Kendra whispered, giving her the hoarse

encouragement that would end this. "It's okay."

Viv gasped, quivering, and came.

Kendra collapsed beside her. Viv made a small, tired sound of happiness and curled into Kendra's arms. They held each other, trusting and safe.

After a little while, Viv's head grew heavy on Kendra's shoulder. Her arms went slack. She seemed to have fallen asleep.

Hmm. Kendra ran a feather-light touch across her back, but Viv didn't stir. All right then. No need to wake her, right? Kendra hugged her closer, adjusted her arm position to be more comfortable, and told her body it was time to sleep.

Some time later, Kendra felt Viv shift in her arms.

"You don't fool me," Viv whispered, barely audible.

Because that's what you did when the person in bed with you was awake. You whispered. So you wouldn't wake them. Uh-huh. Kendra kept her breath even and her eyes closed. Which wasn't hard to do, actually. She really did feel more than half-asleep.

"I know you can hear me," Viv breathed.

She sounded like she meant it, yet she did nothing to try to force Kendra to admit to it. Not like the last time, when she'd tricked Kendra into opening her eyes.

Kendra let out a drowsy sigh. She probably shouldn't be cheating on their last day. But her arms felt heavy and she couldn't remember how to move and maybe that meant she really was asleep?

"I'm going to let you get away with it." Viv brushed a soft kiss on her shoulder.

You don't have to do that, babe.

And Kendra knew no more.

Chapter 13

Day 12+1

KENDRA 5 : VIV 5

Street after street, block after block, their neighborhood had outdone itself with the outdoor Christmas decorations, and Viv insisted that driving by was not enough: they needed to be on foot to admire the pretty lights. In the dark, of course. Together. Several hours after sundown. By which point the temperature had dropped enough that Kendra was forced to admit she should have taken Viv up on her offer to turn back to get her gloves when she realized she'd forgotten them in the house.

Viv had remember her own gloves. And her fuzzy scarf. *And* her hat.

"No earmuffs?" Kendra teased, switching her sippy travel mug of hot cider to her other hand so her bare hands could take turns in her pockets. Unfortunately, the mug was so well-insulated that holding it didn't warm her hands at all.

The smell of coffee and melted candy cane wafted over from Viv's matching travel mug, and Kendra snagged it to steal a sip.

"Drink your own," Viv said.

"Yours tastes better."

"I asked before we left if you wanted coffee and you said no, you wouldn't be able to sleep if you had coffee this late."

"I thought hot cider sounded more Christmas-y," Kendra said, and waited for Miss Accuracy to remind her that Christmas was over.

"Since when do *you* care about things being Christmas-y?"

"You like Christmas-y," Kendra said, like that explained everything. Because it kind of did.

Kendra's hair was tousled from the wind, and Viv removed one of her gloves and reached out to smooth it into place. "It was a good Christmas. We should do this again next year."

"Yeah." Kendra blinked at a yard dotted with illuminated reindeer. Next Christmas sounded depressingly distant. Were they going to fall back into old habits after this? Forget they were allowed to touch each other?

Viv wormed her bare hand into Kendra's coat pocket. She found Kendra's hand, and when she clasped it, Kendra squeezed back, almost afraid to move, because Viv never did this. They were on the sidewalk. Outdoors. Strangers were driving by. Neighbors could see them. If they were looking. Which they probably weren't. But they might.

Viv dangled her glove in Kendra's face. "Put this on."

"I'm okay." Just because they shared a glove size didn't mean she should deprive Viv of being comfortable.

"I can feel your skin. You're cold."

"I don't want *you* to get cold."

"I won't. Your pocket is toasty. Come on. Put it on."

Kendra disentangled herself from the sweet warmth of Viv's hand, passed Viv her mug, and pulled on the glove. Now they each had one hand gloved and one bare. "There we go." She took back her mug and maneuvered Viv's hand back inside her coat pocket, bare hands clasped again and burrowing into the warmth of her coat, and they continued down the street, matching each other's steps with the effortlessness of long familiarity.

Out of the corner of her eye, she saw Viv turn her head in her direction, then away.

"Kendra? I don't want to wait another year."

Kendra drew in a sharp breath.

Inside Kendra's pocket, Viv rubbed her thumb over Kendra's hand.

"Ever heard of the twelve days of Easter?" Viv asked.

Their joined hands flushed with warmth that danced up Kendra's arm to her heart, making her lightheaded. Or possibly the lightheadedness was due to not breathing. She exhaled hard. Didn't help. She inhaled. Yeah, still lightheaded.

Kendra grinned. "Ever heard of I'm not waiting until Easter, are you out of your mind?"

Viv cocked her head like she was considering it. "What about Valentine's Day? That comes before Easter."

"Yeah, I'm not waiting until Valentine's Day, either."

"Well then." Viv's smile blazed with promise. "Who says there are only twelve days of Christmas?"

"We don't have to add days," Kendra said quickly, because seeing her like this was exhilarating, and she didn't want to mess this up. "We'll be going back to real life soon. We could...maybe...enjoy being together without—"

"We don't *have* to," Viv agreed. "But we might *want* to."

"We might?"

Viv pulled her to a stop, and Kendra realized they'd reached home already and she'd been so focused on Viv that she hadn't noticed. Viv led them up their driveway and up the steps to their front door.

"Yesterday was day twelve," Viv said. "I may have to check my math, but I believe that means today is day thirteen." She sipped her coffee, then offered her mug to Kendra. "Here. Have some caffeine."

Kendra ignored the mug and traced Viv's cheekbone with her thumb. "You saying I'm going to need it?"

Viv nuzzled into her touch. "You might."

"And how many days...or nights...will there be?" Kendra cupped the back of her head and kissed her, not needing to hear the answer. Not caring, as long as they were happy together.

Somewhere in between one kiss and the next, Viv whispered, "As many as we want."

About the Author

Siri Caldwell began her career as a hydrogeologist wearing hip-high waders to slog through polluted streams and struggling not to tumble into the water in front of her older, more experienced colleagues. In addition to keeping her balance, she quickly learned that when collecting water samples on farmland and encountering an angry cow, it is best to back away. (Cows: not as docile and picturesque as you'd think.) Now she works at a desk, where the risk of falling or being surprised by interspecies encounters is low and she is not required to wear tall boots of any kind.

When not busy being a dutiful contestant in the rat race, she writes romance novels. Lesbian romance novels—because if anyone knows how to make a relationship complicated, it's a lesbian. And complicated is a good thing on the way to happily ever after.

She lives with her partner outside Washington, DC.

Visit her online at www.siricaldwell.com

Deal-Breaker

Siri Caldwell

2016 Rainbow Awards runner-up

This was not the plan.

After a career-threatening injury, backup dancer Rae Peters crashes at a friend's in a middle-of-nowhere college town to recover. She'd rather be onstage performing with a rock star than stuck in a swimming pool doing rehab exercises, but at least the people-watching is good. Make that person-watching, because she only pays attention to one person: the cute water aerobics instructor who's always lugging around accounting textbooks like she might be smart.

Jori Burgess is a grad student with a young daughter and a blackmailing ex-boyfriend. She's got her hands full being a single mother, and studying, and teaching at the pool, and pretending to be someone she's not. The last thing she needs is one more complication, but Rae is one complication she can't resist.

Rae has no trouble resisting, because she promised herself a long time ago that flirtatious straight girls were not for her. Even if they claimed they weren't that straight. Especially if they claimed they weren't that straight. Really, thank you, but no. She's not going to fall for someone who's got red flags plastered all over her very attractive… uh…personality.

Being friends, though? Being friends is not a problem, and neither is dancing together, and neither is holding on a little longer than is strictly appropriate, and neither is…

Yeah. This could be a problem.

Angel's Touch

Siri Caldwell

2014 Golden Crown Literary Society Award
finalist for Best Debut Novel

Kira has one goal: to make money by opening an exclusive spa in scenic Piper Beach. Megan agrees to help, but money is the last thing on her mind.

Kira Wagner needs a local expert to get her new hotel and spa up and running. Megan McLaren's name is at the top of her list. Megan isn't aware that the woman on her massage table is planning to offer her a job. She gives her healing touch as she would to anyone and turns down the invitation to dinner. But the persistent Kira awakens something else in Megan: memories of pasts they may have shared, none of which ended happily. When Megan realizes exactly where Kira plans to build her hotel, she agrees to consult, but her only goal is to make sure the new hotel doesn't ruin the sacred space nearby. She wishes she could tell Kira the truth, but she's deeply afraid that Kira will look at her like every other woman in her life when she explains about the powerful ley lines…and the angels…

Earth Angel

Siri Caldwell

New England Chapter, Romance Writers of America
Readers' Choice Award finalist for
Best Contemporary Romance of 2013

People say Abby Vogel sounds like an angel when she plays her harp at weddings and other events in beautiful Piper Beach. They don't need to know that real angels—or possibly figments of her imagination—keep her company. They wouldn't understand.

Gwynne Abernathy blames herself for the deaths of her sister and mother. Her psychic gifts have brought her only grief, and she's turned her back on anything that isn't "normal". Abby's kindness and quirkiness are irresistible, but there must be a reason Abby is swarmed by angels, and she suspects that when she discovers it she'll want to stay far, far away.

Abby knows immediately that there is more to Gwynne than meets the eye. When she realizes she's not the only one who sees angels—that Gwynne sees them, too—she finally trusts that her glowing friends are not hallucinations. What's more, the angels desperately need something from her. If she answers their call, it means giving up the magic she feels with Gwynne. It means giving up…everything.

CPSIA information can be obtained
at www.ICGtesting.com
Printed in the USA
FSHW01n2243200618
49646FS